SKIN DEEP

Scholastic Australia
An imprint of Scholastic Australia Pty Limited
PO Box 579 Gosford NSW 2250
ABN 11 000 614 577
www.scholastic.com.au

Part of the Scholastic Group
Sydney • Auckland • New York • Toronto • London • Mexico City
New Delhi • Hong Kong • Buenos Aires • Puerto Rico

Published by Scholastic Australia in 2021.

Cover illustrations: Anna Ismagilova/Shutterstock.com; Umy Art/Shutterstock.com; wrongorright/Shutterstock.com; photolinc/Shutterstock.com.
Designed by Elly Whiley.

A catalogue record for this book is available from the National Library of Australia

ISBN: 978-1-76097-644-6

Typeset in ITC Berkeley Oldstyle, Shartoll Light, Shockwave SANS, Gloria Hallelujah, Helvetica Neue and Adobe Jenson.

Printed in China by Hang Tai Printing Company Limited.

This product is made of material from well-managed FSC®-certified forests, recycled material, and other controlled sources.

10 9 8 7 6 5 4 3 2 1 24 25 26 27 28 / 2

For my incredible little women, Mia, Zara, Sophie, Heidi and Lacey:
In a world that seeks to define you by beauty, clothe yourselves
in strength. It lasts a lifetime.

And for Karen O'Connor:
Little did I know the day I was born, just how lucky I was. I got
to be your daughter, and call the most wondrous woman my
mother. You have my heart, my love, my respect, always.

HAYLEY LAWRENCE

A Scholastic Australia book

ONE

Miss French wants us to write what we are most scared of. This is a good way to start a story, she says. So Henry writes about vampires and Mia about a ghost in her bedroom cupboard. Ella writes of dying and Zeke about being abducted. My page remains blank.

'She's scared of fire,' Pippi says, in her know-it-all way.

Because, of course, I should be. But the truth is, I remember the flames. I felt them licking my skin. But it was only when I squinted open my eyes to a white, buzzing room that I felt the pain. Burning, gnawing pain across my face, my chest, my stomach, my arms. But pain is different—very different—to fear, isn't it?

It wasn't until I heard Gran catch a sob in her hand and say, 'She was so beautiful,' that I understood what it means to be scared.

So what am I most scared of? No, Pippi, it's not fire. It's ugliness. And that is something I don't need to write about. It's already written across my face.

I ignore Pippi, the way I always ignore the comments. I put my head down and write.

My tutu is splayed, my heart pounding, pointe shoes ribboned to my knees, my toes aching. The audience is a dark, fearsome pool before me. They want perfection. When you're dancing to Swan Lake, there's no room for the wrong step. The music darts across the stage, and my toes dart with it in synchronised points. My hair is slicked back in a bun, my mouth smiling, ever smiling. Sometimes, I feel like a circus clown. Performing, juggling, face painted into a smile. And not only when I'm dancing.

I stop writing.

I never used to feel like a circus clown. Not before. But there are a lot of things I feel now that I never felt in the *before*.

The *after* is a place I wish I had never visited, not even for a minute. The kind of haunting nightmare you want to shake off, and carry on your normal day without.

But the *after* is my forever.

When your face wears your story and your story isn't pretty, there's really nowhere to hide it. My scars aren't like Miss French's tattoo of a butterfly that sometimes pokes a wing out from the back of her singlet when she's writing on the whiteboard. My scars aren't like the 'shark bite' Anna got on her leg last summer—not a real shark bite, the kind she got when she put her foot through a glass shower-screen door, which everyone says is really cool.

Scars on your face aren't cool. I learnt that very fast, in the hospital, with the doctor. With the words, 'this is very delicate', and 'given she's a girl', and 'there are some wonderful concealers available', and 'she's a very pretty girl—we'll get the best guy for the job'. Of course, Dad snapped at him, 'I'd hope you'd get the best guy for the job no matter how pretty she was!' And, of course, the doctor apologised then. But it was too late. Maybe he just spoke what others only dared to think?

Thankfully Miss French isn't like that doctor. She's the kind with shiny eyes, who eats words like chocolate cake and then delivers them back to us as mousse. She doesn't talk much about faces, only about stories and characters and epic battles. Every Friday afternoon, we get to put our heads down on our desks, feel the lazy fan buffeting our hair and listen to her voice as she reads us the classics: *The Secret Garden*, *Anne of Green Gables*, *Narnia*. It's my favourite hour. But today is not a Friday.

The buzzer goes for lunch. I haven't finished my piece of writing.

'Fold your papers up, please, write your name on the front and leave them on my desk on your way out,' Miss French says. 'Wait till you see what I get you to do with these beauties!'

I'm usually one of her best students, and I hate disappointing Miss French, so I scrawl a little 'Sorry' at the bottom of my piece. As I file out of class, I drop my folded sheet on top of Anna's.

'The shark bite's pink today,' Byron says, studying Anna's leg.

'That means I'm warm. It's my thermostat,' Anna says. 'Pink when I'm warm, purple when I'm cold.'

'Cool.'

'Harry Potter had a cool scar,' Miss French says. Everyone in the line snaking out the door stops and turns to look at her. Everyone except me.

She means on his face. Like me.

She could be saying this for Byron. He has scars on his face too. But his look almost like dimples now. He likes to tell the story of how, when he was a baby, a dog latched onto his cheek. He calls it his battle wound; like it somehow makes him brave, even though he doesn't remember anything about the attack.

But I know Miss French is saying this for my benefit. Trying to give me a literary hero to cling to.

'Scars are just like tattoos,' Miss French continues. 'Except they have more exciting backstories.'

Nobody seems to know what to say to this, so they keep walking, me on their heels, bursting to get into a different airspace. Far away from scar talk.

I pity Miss French. She tries hard to make me feel okay. As hard as she possibly can. But a lightning bolt on your forehead is still cool. And Harry was cute, at least in the movies. Not to mention a wizard, who defeated Voldemort. If I only had wizardry or cuteness or a petite little scar with a fascinating story connected to my mother dying . . . maybe then I'd have a hope.

Miss French doesn't yet know what I know: it will never be okay. There's no point pretending. The *after* is my forever. I have to learn to live inside the nightmare. I could have battled the devil himself, and it wouldn't matter. Because nobody sees the battle; they only see the ugliness it left behind.

I can talk about the *before* with my friends. I can even talk about the *after* a little.

Those aren't the bits they're interested in, though.

Not the twenty-two skin grafts or the nine infections or the thirteen surgeries or the organ failure. Not the donor skin or the pressure suits or the learning to swallow again or the ongoing physiotherapy or the boxing sessions with Dad every morning.

Since I came back to school, the only part my friends want to know about is the bridge between the *before* and the *after*. But 'bridge' isn't really the right word, is it? Because bridges are built to mend distances. What happened to me didn't fix anything; it only destroyed everything. Dad calls it my war. He says soldiers come home from war and don't tell everyone what they saw or what they did, and I don't have to either.

But my friends still want my story. Pippi told me she *needed* to know. I *needed* to tell everyone so they could understand. And I've learnt that if I don't give people my story, they do a scrappy job of piecing it together themselves.

Imagination can't always do justice to the truth.

The last microseconds replay in my head over and over, in slow motion fragments. The screech of metal. A spinning sensation. Twirling like a carnival ride. The silence. The explosion.

These are the tiny details my friends hunger for. So they can gasp and cover their pretty mouths.

It's the story I will never tell them. The story nobody knows I remember.

My psychologist, Nikki, says that when something unimaginably bad happens to us, our bodies do this amazing thing: they forget. They don't let our minds remember.

But I remember. I remember every single second in astonishing detail. Details I keep locked inside the vault of my mind where nobody is allowed entry, not even me.

I follow Anna and the group into the glary sunshine, and pull my wide-brimmed hat low over my eyes. My skin will have to be covered from the sun for at least the next year.

Anna makes room for me in the circle as we sit down, the way she's always done. We pretend things are the same as they always were, but, of course, they're not.

Sandwiches and fruit and frozen drinks are brought out in our circle on the grass. The girls trade a finger bun for a packet of chips, a muesli bar for a cheese snack, a cupcake for a fruit cup.

Pippi beckons everyone to lean in. She looks around conspiratorially.

'So I heard a little rumour yesterday about Oscar Jabore. Oscar and Summer.'

My heart thuds dully. Oscar's family goes camping by the River Tweed every year. And every year, he's allowed to bring a friend. Last year, I was that friend. Of course, I didn't go in the end. While he was threading fishing lines with worms and casting along the river, I was fighting an infection that sent my heart racing and almost killed me.

I try not to remember last summer. There weren't many nice days in it. I'm not even sure what a nice day is made of anymore. A day that doesn't involve surgery is nice. One that doesn't include pain is nice too. One where I don't cry. Or want to hide in my room.

I say I need the bathroom and leave the group talking about summer camps, while I escape to the sterile, white-tiled girls' toilet block. Lock myself in the third cubicle along. Sit down on the toilet and breathe slowly. Small spaces, slow breathing, solitude: these are my key coping strategies. The toilet door is a graveyard of old thoughts. I pass over the tags about Summer loving Jasper forever and Sophie being BFFs with Anna. It's the words in the top right-hand corner that always bring me comfort. Thick purple marker. Chunky block letters.

YESTERDAY MATTERED YESTERDAY

No name attached, no tag. I want to know who the words belong to. What happened that brought a girl to write them.

Oscar was going to ask me to be his girlfriend on that camping trip. If his friend, Byron, is to be believed. I'm very glad he didn't. Because I'd have said yes. And things would have become very awkward for him afterwards. How do you dump a girl when she's been burnt? I'd have had to dump him, I guess. I'd rather live the rest of my days alone than with someone's pity.

YESTERDAY MATTERED YESTERDAY

Breathe in slowly, breathe out slowly.

In slowly, out slowly.

In, out.

It works. My heartbeat slows to a flutter.

I flush the toilet I didn't use and leave the cubicle. Then I face the row of taps at the basin.

Eyes up, Scarlett.

Three . . . two . . . one. Do it.

I drag my eyes up to confront the mirror. Hold them there.

Stare at the stranger-face. The mask I had to wear for months in the *after* was better than the stranger-face. It was a shield. There's nothing to hide behind now. A face can't be covered with clothes.

Harry Potter's scar was a lightning bolt on his forehead. It's almost a cop-out. Plus, he's a boy. Hermione wasn't scarred. She got to be clever *and* beautiful.

I'm the girl who lived. The real one. Minus the magic. With scars stretching jagged fingers up my face.

I trace the puckered skin that snakes up my neck, reaching around my right eye, through what's left of my eyebrow and into my hairline. Thick and fascinatingly unfamiliar. This face isn't mine. The real Scarlett's skin is porcelain, and she has a white-blonde hairline that meets at a devil's peak in the front of her forehead. I need to find a way back to the real me. Maybe if I have enough plastic surgery, if they playdough my skin back into the right shape, one day, I'll look at my face again and think, 'Aha, there she is! I found her!'

Scarlett is pretty. Scarlett is beautiful. Scarlett is gorgeous. Scarlett is stunning. Choose any of those familiar words.

Just not ugly.

'Ugly' comes from an Old Norse word that meant 'to dread', but the dictionary says it means 'unpleasant to look at; offensive to beauty'.

Is my face so offensive? I want to tear the word 'ugly' out of all dictionaries. Remove it from every search engine. So nobody has to know what it means, or, worse, how it feels.

In the *before*, 'ugly' was a word I used. One I didn't understand. One I had never experienced. I wasn't meant to be joined to that word. Not everyone gets to be pretty, I know that. It's good luck or good genes or both. But I had the lucky combination. I wasn't born like this. My face brought smiles from old ladies in the street. My body brought claps from crowds when I danced. My long golden hair just asked for hands to braid it.

Now I am without braids and claps and smiles. I don't even know what I am anymore. The nasty voice in the back of my head whispers, *Maybe you're a monster?*

I want to hunt down my old life, gather its pieces in my mottled hands and put it back together. I want to walk through the schoolyard without stares. I want pool parties with Anna. I want Byron sending me messages on social media to tell me Oscar has a crush on me. I want to feel my smooth, unbroken skin beneath my fingertips. I want sunshine splashing my face without my skin burning up. I want to un-know what surgery feels like, and what a skin graft means, and whether the skin graft will be another big useless failure. I want to un-know the smell of hospital antiseptic. I want to dance without being studied for all the wrong reasons.

I miss the words more than I can tell anyone. Pretty. Beautiful. Gorgeous. Stunning. I miss those words so much it hurts. I have lost countless hot tears lying in bed at night for the words I will never be again. No matter how many surgeries or grafts or plastic surgeons I put up with. My face is like Humpty Dumpty: all the king's horses and all the king's men couldn't put me back together again.

We all have scars; some of us carry them inside, some outside. That's what Nikki tells me. Except some people carry both.

I turn my face to the good side, where the burns only licked at my jawline and up half my cheek. I look almost pretty. Almost. But then I turn to the other side.

Cruel words leap inside my brain. That nasty little voice in the back of my head whispers to me again. *Monster*.

Nikki says monsters are human creations. Monsters only live in our minds.

But I've seen the picture on her desk. Two perfect, smiling children. She can't know much about looking like a monster. Even in *Beauty and the Beast*, there was a spell to transform the beast. The spell was true love. Fairytales don't pretend it's okay. It was not okay for the monster to stay monstrous. He had to become beautiful.

I splash water on my face and pat it dry. Then I take a lungful of air and push the bathroom door open into the glare of the day.

By the time I get back to the group, Anna's talking about a pool party at her place. I wish I'd stayed in the bathroom a bit longer. Long enough to miss the invitation. But there it is.

'Scarlett, you'll come?' She looks at me, her bronze eyes big and earnest.

Anna remembers how much I loved pool parties in the *before*. I remember too. The small leap of my heart over long, lazy days mermaiding in her pool. We don't have a pool at home—too much maintenance, Dad says, when the beach is just down the road. But a pool is an entirely different experience to a beach, isn't it? A pool is warm, and safe to dive into without fear of sharks or rips or rough swells. So Anna and I could spend all day in her pool, dragging ourselves out when we got too cold and roasting our tummies on the sunbaked pavers. Until our skin burned and we dived back into the deep end with a scream. Repeated over and over until the sun sank, the shadows grew long enough to bathe our bodies, our teeth began to chatter and warm showers lured us inside.

But the thought of a group pool party in the *after*?

My heart flutters with panic. She may as well be asking me to swim naked.

Everyone in the circle is looking at me. My mind blanks. I can't think of a single excuse to wriggle out of it. Not one.

Time slows. The eyes on me grow larger with each second. My good armpit prickles with sweat.

I make the mistake of locking gazes with Pippi. Her speckled eyes are as smug as a cat's. Is she enjoying this? Watching me squirm?

'You can come next time if you don't feel up to it,' Anna says.

She must be able to see me drowning before her. The whole group must. But it's Pippi's shiny eyes that decide it for me.

'I'll come,' I say casually. 'Of course I'll come. When?'

'This afternoon.'

I smile and scoff the rest of my lunch. It goes down like a stone in my stomach.

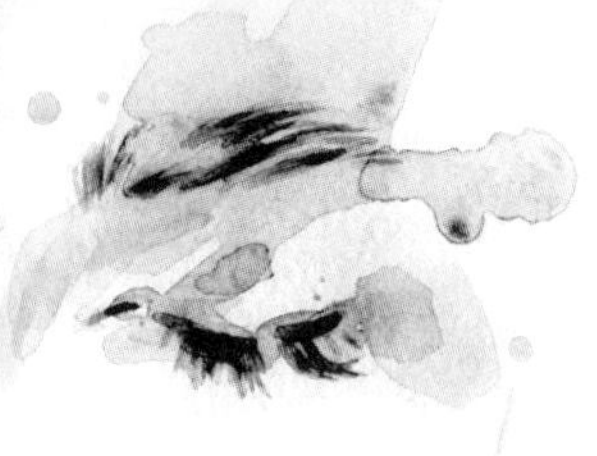

BEFORE

My stomach zips with butterflies as Gran ties the laces on my slippers. They feel tight on my feet.

I run in, my skirt flowing out behind me.

'Have fun, my little princess,' Gran says.

I feel like a real ballerina.

There are mirrors on every wall.

I like watching myself. I look like my ballerina doll.

The whole room is full of ballerina dolls.

Gran watches from her corner in the room.

Miss Rachel paces the floor. We all stand a little stiffer as she passes.

Miss Rachel doesn't smile much. Her chest is pushed out, her toes pointed. She walks like a tall bird with stick legs.

My heart beats harder everytime she stalks past me.

'Hold the barre, children, and bend down, then up. Good.' Miss Rachel looks around, watching us all do what she's shown us. My skirt billows like a jellyfish as I bend my knees out.

'And again. Down, up. Beautiful, Scarlett!'

I look at Gran. She's watching me, a small smile on her lips. Gran is very happy when I dance.

Almost as happy as me.

TWO

Anna is happier than me when she opens her front door. I stand there, clutching a limp bag I threw a few things into at the last minute. My stomach churns, and my mouth waters in response. If I speak one word, I might vomit into the ferns edging her front porch.

So I don't speak. I let Anna guide me inside. I don't take my hat off, or my sunnies. It's safer hiding.

Anna guides me through her family's living room and kitchen, where her mum is cutting carrot sticks and watermelon. She puts the knife down as we approach.

'Scarlett, darling, so good to see you,' her mum says in that tone. I know she's being kind, but it reeks of pity. 'How are you?'

'Good.'

Always the same answer. Good. *Life is good. Everything is fine. I'm adaptable. Please stop looking at me like that. Let's pretend this is normal, because pretending is all I've got right now.*

But her mum doesn't pretend. She steps out from behind the kitchen bench, and, before I can do anything about it, wraps me in a bear hug.

'I've missed seeing you,' she says, squeezing me against her soft chest. 'You come here anytime you like. Even if it's just you and Anna. Anytime, okay? You're always welcome, darling.'

'Okay, Mum, that's enough,' Anna says. She mouths 'sorry' at me from behind her mum's back and her mum lets me go.

'I don't mean to embarrass you, darling. But you know you have our support.'

'Thank you,' I say, straightening my now crooked sunglasses.

I feel her eyes on me as we head for the backyard. Already I can hear splashing and squealing. They're in there. The pool.

And I'm dressed for the part. In my own swimmers, pretending I'm going to join them. Except even my swimmers make me stand out. How many fourteen-year-olds strut around in a full-sleeved rash shirt? And tell me exactly how many fourteen-year-olds look good in a wide-brimmed hat?

Anna peels back the sliding door and we step out onto her back deck, which overlooks the pool and garden down below.

It's worse than I'd feared. I'd assumed it was a girls-only deal. Somewhere, maybe when I was hiding out in the bathroom, I missed the detail about the boys coming.

Oscar and Byron are resting back, elbows on towels in their boardshorts, cool as a pair of crocodiles. Sunnies on, hair wet, skin perfect. There's splashing and shrieking from the pool, and a flash of red hair tells me it's Pippi, along with maybe Amber. Summer and Tyra are lying carelessly on their tummies on towels sprawled by the paved edge of the pool. They're in two-piece swimmers, which show off their perfect skin. Tyra's is a bright, froggy green, a stark contrast against her tan, and Summer's is hot pink, which sets off her blonde hair.

Anna leads me down the stairs and I follow, my legs filled with stones, getting heavier with every step. The boys look up as we approach.

'Hey,' they say.

For once, I'm thankful for my need to avoid direct sunlight. And Anna has a spot set up for me under the gazebo at the far end of her pool, where big colourful cushions are scattered beneath the shade of its thatched roof. She sits with me and I feel safer out of the bright glare of the sun. We watch the boys get up from their towels and run towards the pool in unison, taking flying leaps and tucking their knees under their arms as they bomb-dive in next to the girls, splashing us all. When Oscar breaks through the water, laughing and shaking his hair, Pippi slaps him.

'Dude, you scared me,' she says.

What is Pippi scared of? A boy bomb-diving into the pool beside her. I smirk to myself.

I watch Amber stand by the side of the pool, raising her muscled arms either side of her ears. Her tanned skin is taut and glistens in the sun as she dives gracefully into the choppy surface of the water, piercing it with her fingers, before being swallowed into it. Summer follows her. Six careless bodies splashing in Anna's pool. Don't they see how perfect they are?

I am aware of the ugliness of my long-sleeved rash shirt. Gran bought it for me because I refused to go shopping with her for one. She wanted to get me something bright and girly. I said to get black. Plain black. I'm not looking to attract attention.

A game of tag starts up in the pool. Lots of laughter, splashing, noise. I tell Anna to go join them.

'You won't come?' she says.

'Nah, I'm good here,' I say.

I mean it. I'm happier watching. Even though I crave the cool water against my sweaty skin, I'm happier in my shady hideout. Without the pressure of people looking at me or tiptoeing around me, I can relax into their game. Even laugh, like I do when Oscar lunges for Amber and she slips to one side. He misses her by a fingernail.

I watch as Pippi gets cornered. She screams when Oscar touches her. Then I watch Pippi catch Tyra, and Tyra get Summer, and Summer catch Byron. I can do this. I can be at a pool party. This is not as bad as I'd imagined.

'Okay, guys!' Anna's mum is standing on the deck, looking down over the pool. 'I have food for the hungry. Sausage rolls, party pies, fruit and veggies. Come and get it!'

The boys scramble out of the pool like they've been starved for a week. The girls follow, picking up their towels and wrapping them around their bodies, jewelled with water droplets. The boys don't even bother with towels, they just drip up the stairs, shivering, their skin tight with gooseflesh. Dark skin, light skin and everything-in-between skin—all of it painfully perfect.

I follow at the back, the only dry one. We fill our plates with food and eat under the shade of the deck.

Anna's mum reappears with a jug of water, some cups. Everyone mumbles their thanks.

'Okay, while I've got you all together,' she says. 'Let's do a group photo.'

My heart stops beating. Group photo? For what? Her social media? I don't do photos. Not even with my family. I know what this is about. It'll be one of those perfect happy snaps. What a perfect mum she is hosting this perfect party in her perfect house for her perfect daughter. And people will see me. Notice me. They'll secretly tell Anna's mum how kind she is to look after me. And she is kind. But I don't want to be part of an advertisement for her perfect life. It's very clear I don't belong.

But there's no time to say no. Or make a fuss.

My stomach is weak and sick. I can no longer eat any of the food on my plate. I push my hat down low over my face as she tells us to smile.

'Big smiles, that's it!'

I don't smile. Can't. I can only hope my hat is jammed low enough to create some shade over my face. Make me unrecognisable.

We head back to the pool area after the photo session.

On our way down, I hear Summer telling Tyra she wants to lose weight. She's already thin, but she doesn't like 'these bits' on her thighs. She keeps her towel wrapped around her tummy. Pippi says, 'At least you're not freckly like me, Summer. Not much you can do with this many freckles.' Anna says she wants to steal Tyra's tan, make herself less pale. 'Just some of it. I'll leave you some, I swear.'

Their perfection is wasted on them.

I say nothing about what I would change. What I would swap with them. With anyone.

When we get down to the grass, things get worse.

The girls start pulling out their phones. Anna's mum has started something.

'Group selfie! C'mon, guys!' Tyra calls.

I slink off to my shadows in the gazebo.

'Scarlett, c'mon,' Tyra says.

But I can't tolerate another second of photos.

'Nah, I'm good,' I say.

An awkward silence falls over the group on the grass.

'We don't need photos,' Anna says. 'We have our memories.'

Oh, Anna, please don't. She's trying so hard to make it okay. I just want them to carry on and ignore me.

'Okay, just one then,' Tyra says. 'Oscar, Byron, get your butts in here.'

Everyone gathers behind Tyra. I watch them out of the corner of my eye, the girls posing with air kisses, the boys doing cool hand gestures as she clicks. Not once, but probably a dozen times. To give her a selection of photos. So she can scan through later and find the one that makes her look the best. I know. I used to do it too.

Then she'll pick a cute filter for the photo, to add sparkles, or butterflies, or hearts. It will make their teeth whiter, their skin clearer, their eyes brighter, their lashes thicker, their faces slimmer. On social media, the group will be animation-style perfect. Not a pimple, not a mark, not a blemish to be seen.

I have tried the same filters on my face. Just to see what they might do.

Not enough. Filters aren't designed to fix my level of blemish. And even if they were, none of it's real. In real life, there are no sparkles, no butterflies, no hearts. There are pimples, and scars, and braces, and dimpled thighs, and teeth not always glowing white. Hello, we're fourteen. The perfect confident self only exists in the online space. The one we move around in on Earth, that's the real self. The one that has to face school, shopping, teachers, friends and doctors.

I scroll through my phone so that I don't look like a total loner in the gazebo by myself. But it's not too long before Anna and Pippi join me. The others are lying on their towels on the pavers, sunning themselves like water dragons by a lagoon.

'Ugh, I wish I could stay at your place next week,' Pippi moans to Anna.

'What's so bad about yours?'

'Nothing, if I was actually staying at mine. But Dad got this idea that we all need to go on a digital detox or some crap. In the middle of nowhere in the country. He doesn't realise the only reason he got the idea for a digital detox was from something he watched online in the first place.'

Anna grimaces. 'Maybe you could just sneak your phone into your bag, use it on the sly?'

Pippi shakes her head. 'No point. It's like, so remote out there, there's no network coverage. No wi-fi even. Nothing at all to do. Not another soul within yelling distance. Just dirt and grass and hills. Completely disconnected. Like something out of hell.'

That's when I get my idea.

It doesn't involve pool parties. Or selfies. Or Oscar Jabore. Or anyone else.

It doesn't even involve becoming beautiful again.

It just requires letting go.
Of absolutely everything.

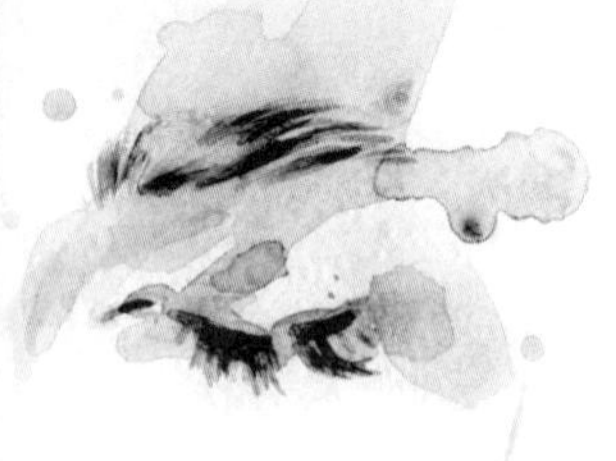

BEFORE

Absolutely everything has led to this moment.

In this studio with its mirrored walls, I am showcased. Every point of my toes, every sweep of my hands, captured by ceiling to floor mirrors that don't leave any room for mistakes.

I slide on my slippers, and pad to the middle of the studio.

'First position,' Miss Alisha says. 'And Scarlett, remember the story this piece is telling. Dancing isn't just about movement, it's about storytelling. Don't be lazy.'

The piece of music is Bird Set Free, *about a girl who can't sing anymore, who holds in all her music until the day it explodes out of her.*

I eye myself in the mirror. Hair pulled high into a slick golden bun, trapped inside a net, not one hair out of place.

Solo recitals are tougher than group dances. There's nowhere to hide. But my exam is next week, so I need to get this right.

I curl myself into a ball on the shiny wooden floor. Wait for Miss Alisha to cue the music. Count myself into its beat.

On the fourth beat, I snake out my arms, twist my body up to its full height, then leap. Toes pointing, skirt floating out like a parachute,

landing softly across the room, like a deer.

I spin down to my knees, stretching out in time with the music, first to one side, then to the other, until I'm up again and reaching for the stars. My body moves in and out, around and about, small and crunched, then long and graceful. I sway and dart and pull myself around the studio. Use the space, own the space.

I am part of the music, like a willow tree swaying in the wind. The wind is the music and I am the tree, blown by her sound.

The music slowly dies, and my dancing dies with it, until I am sitting back on the floor in front of Miss Alisha, knees bent, toes pointed, chest lifted to the ceiling, my head thrown back dramatically behind me.

Miss Alisha claps. 'Beautiful,' she says. 'Beautiful work, Scarlett. If you can do that for the exam next week, you'll pass. Keep up the practise.'

I skip out of my solo without taking off my ballet slippers and barely feel the ground beneath me. Miss Alisha doesn't dish out many compliments.

Gran's SUV is hovering in the carpark, lights on, engine running, ready to grab me and head to soccer training to collect my brother.

I breathe a lungful of cool evening air and run fairy-like to the passenger seat, skirt billowing as I open the door and spring inside.

'I'm ready,' I tell her.

THREE

I'm ready. I burst through our glass-slatted front door, dump my bag at the foot of the staircase and make for the study. I find exactly who I'm looking for, frowning at her laptop screen. She scrolls down, gulping the last of her tea.

'All I need is a mountain,' I say.

Gran jumps and a splash of tea lands on her cream shirt. 'Scarlett, don't sneak up on me like that!'

'Sorry, but that's all I need. A mountain.'

'A what?' She scrubs at her shirt with a tissue. 'Why are you panting like that?' Touches her phone screen. 'Good grief, it's five o'clock.'

Gran pushes away from her laptop and heads for the kitchen.

'Danny!' she calls up the stairs.

I follow her. 'A mountain and a cabin, Gran. That's all I need.'

She grabs a water bottle from the fridge, a banana from the fruit bowl. 'Is this for Geography?' Then she turns for the stairs again and yells, 'Danny, we're running late!'

Okay, so the afternoon mania is a bad time to hit Gran with

the news. But since I quit dancing, it's only Danny she has to run around after, and I actually can't wait hours for her to get home. It's bursting out of me. It's the answer. I just need her to agree.

'I need a forest full of trees.'

'Danny, if I have to come up there!'

'A pack of dogs for company.'

'Is this some kind of riddle? Sweetie, can we do this later?'

'Maremma Sheepdogs. Smiley and loyal. Guardians of the flock.'

A plan isn't a plan without the research. Gran will appreciate my research.

'Sweetie, I have no idea what you're on about, but we'll finish this when—Danny!'

'I'm coming, alright!' My brother's voice cracks. 'Hold onto your hair, geez.'

He thumps down the stairs like a giraffe.

'Gran, I just need us to get away for a bit,' I say. 'Please?'

'Get away?' Danny says. 'Away where?'

'To a mountain. By ourselves. Just for a bit.'

Danny rolls his eyes. 'I'm not going to any mountain. I have soccer finals.'

He grabs an apple from the fruit bowl, tosses it in the air and catches it in his mouth. Takes a big juicy bite.

'Well, lucky you,' I say.

Danny, whose life goes on just as before.

Danny, who was spared the accident. The fire. The scars.

'Life's not just about . . .' But he backs down before he says the words. *Princess Scarlett*. Those are old words. The biggest insult he could dish out in the *before*. Scarlett the princess. Now I'd think it was a compliment to be called a princess.

He takes another bite of his apple before Gran reefs him out the door by his shoulder. A rush of wind goes with them as the door closes and seals me in. Silence. A pang of disappointment.

Gran doesn't listen anymore. It's been more than twelve months. It's time for life to chug back into gear. And it has for her. For Danny. For Dad. Just not for me.

Dad's not due home for an hour, so I settle myself on our suede lounge, tuck my legs up under my skirt, and peer out onto our neat little street with its pressed green lawns. Houses with white shuttered windows and white fences, small shiny cars nosed up against panelled garage doors. I like street watching. The thin slats in our plantation shutters keep the world out, so I can watch it without it always watching me back.

I'm only ever okay like this. World out, me in.

Monsters belong far away from the busy world of normal people. Not for the sake of everyone else, but for the sake of themselves. Let me live in peace. Unwatched. Get me out of this glass fishbowl where I swim laps day after day before the googly eyes of other kids. If I wasn't always being watched, observed, talked about, reminded of the face I wear, I *could* be okay. I could let go of words like 'pretty' and I could care a whole lot less about words like 'ugly'. Ugly is only a curse so long as people are there to see it, think it, say it. Dogs don't care about ugly. They care about kind touches and warm words and long walks. Dogs don't care about pool parties or social media feeds or how many followers you have or how many likes you get on a post. They don't care if your scars are raging red from the heat or purple from the cold.

If I don't find a way to escape soon, I *will* die. Not on the outside, on the inside. And that's the worst kind of death.

I don't want a mountain; I *need* one.

I haven't decided on the exact spot yet. I'm still narrowing my options. Somewhere between the Great Dividing Range and the western ranges. The more desolate, the better.

I could live surprisingly simply off the land. If I could just give up lollies and chocolate. And if I can talk Gran and Dad into moving out of our white-rendered house, where nobody really talks about anything that matters. From this perfectly groomed neighbourhood of perfectly groomed houses with perfectly groomed rose bushes and parents who whiz their perfect kids from school to soccer to dental appointments to ballet to boxing.

If I'd been living a simple life on a mountain, the accident would never have happened in the first place. If I had a mother to whiz me to dancing like everybody else, instead of a tired old gran, maybe she'd have reacted faster and the accident wouldn't have been as bad.

Gran hasn't even apologised. I know it wasn't technically her fault. But she was driving. She was making the decisions.

It was exactly because of the afternoon mania that I was sitting in that car to begin with. When you're racing from soccer to ballet, there's no time for a toilet stop, no time for a delay. There was no time for a car accident in our afternoon schedule. Certainly not the kind where a squad of ambulances and police cars and fire trucks rock up. The kind that shuts down a main road and makes everyone else late too. Doctors, vets, plumbers, artists, officeworkers. It didn't matter who they were, they were all going to be late that afternoon.

Car accidents don't care if you've got a ballet exam starting in five minutes. Accidents like that wipe every thought of ballet clean from your mind to the point where you forget you're even a dancer. Or why you were rushing to begin with.

In the *before*, the exam felt ultra-important. Quick, quick, rush, rush. In the *after*, I wish we'd been five minutes late. One minute late. Thirty seconds late. Skipped the exam. Been sick that day. Forgotten about it. Anything except being in the wrong place at exactly the wrong second with Gran.

Now Gran's back to the rushing with Danny. Like she's forgotten what can happen. Like she's forgotten she didn't respond fast enough to the danger. Or what that cost me.

The lawyers haven't forgotten. I hope the truck driver hasn't forgotten either. Because the lawyers agreed he was the one who mostly caused the accident. And because of that, his insurance company will have to pay me. Dad and Gran don't talk to me much about the court case, but I know it's being fought behind the scenes. And I have to go and see doctors so they can write reports about me. All the things I can and can't do. Now and forever. It's why I talk to Nikki too. Not just to help me adjust to my new life, but also so she can write up reports and send those to the lawyers to show just how much the accident has screwed up my mind. Made me depressed and anxious or whatever. To show how much that truck driver harmed my mind and my body.

Because it turns out that if you take away a girl's prettiness, you have to pay for it. How much is that worth? How much should a truck driver have to pay for a lifetime of scars on a young girl? I know it's not really just about the scars. It's about the damage to the muscles on my arms too. But, sometimes, it feels like it's all about my face.

The lawyers have talked to me about the things I wanted to do before the accident and can't do anymore. They tell me they need to figure out what I've lost, so they ask what I wanted to be when I grow up. I say a dancer. I wanted to be a dancer. It's the only thing I breathed, dreamt and had any talent in. But now, with my arms so weak, I can't be a ballerina. Ballerinas need muscle, they need strength. Maybe I'll never even be able to dance for myself after this.

What is a lifetime of dancing worth? How much does a dancer make over their whole career? Would I have been an incredible dancer who toured the world, or just an average one nobody ever really knew? Then there are my scars. How much is the loss of beauty worth? How much for an aching heart? How much for a bleeding mind? As if any sum of money can even make up for these things. As if it can buy me back my happiness. I know they're talking lots of money. Hundreds of thousands of dollars kind of money. Enough to buy me some perfectly soulless house in some perfectly soulless street, where I can live the rest of my days without dancing or beauty.

I don't want it. Their money. I don't want to accept the exchange: my happiness for hundreds of thousands of dollars. But Dad says I need to take what they're offering. The surgeries, the medical care, the rehab; it all costs money. I need to be looked after, today and all of my tomorrows. Especially if they're not the kind of tomorrows I wanted.

I agree that I need to be looked after. And I need to start looking after myself better. Which is why I know my mountain idea is a winner.

I can either stay here crying every night and dreading every day, or I can do something about it. Dig a new life from the bottom of this pit. Nobody can save me from myself, so I need creative solutions. At school, they call it 'dynamic problem solving'. Well, my solution *is* dynamic. Unusual. A radical solution for a radical new life.

And for the first time in the *after*, I feel okay. Because soon, if everything goes to plan, I will disappear from here like a plume of smoke, far from anyone who knows me. People will say, 'Remember that girl who got burnt in that car?' I'll be reduced to a nameless, damaged thing. A forgettable horror story.

I jump online and get to work. Narrow down my mountain.

By the time Dad buzzes up the garage door, I'm all prepped and ready for him.

Spread around me on the dining table are printouts, notes, even some sketches. I haven't worked this hard on a project since the ballet exam I never got to do. Gran and Dad keep pushing me to dance again, but they don't understand. My arms can't move the way they once could. They're stiff and restricted by muscle loss and scar tissue. Dancing is about beauty and grace. Dancing will never be mine again.

This, though? This can be mine.

Gran will be impressed by the detail, the research. Dad will be impressed by the drawings, the passion. I just need to talk them both into the idea.

The door to the garage opens. Dad's heavy footfalls come up the hall into the kitchen, where he stops. Sniffs the air. Assesses the table.

I am poised and waiting. Instant coffee for him, exactly the way he likes it: skim milk with half a sugar. Tea for me, white with two sugars. A choc-caramel biscuit for each of us.

'This looks official,' he says.

'I need to talk to you. About something important.'

He lays his keys down alongside the fruit bowl, gives me a kiss on the forehead, then pulls back the chair next to mine and sits, legs apart, face open. Dad will listen. He always listens.

'I need you to keep an open mind. Don't say no straight away.'

He leans back in his chair, takes a sip of coffee. Leaves his biscuit untouched. I can't touch either my tea or my biscuit. My heart has pushed a lump up my throat.

'I've decided I want to go away. All of us to go away, actually. A tree change.'

He blinks a couple of times. Says nothing.

I pull together some pictures. 'I've been researching remote properties. The country thing, you know—living off the land, having your own space, maybe even a few animals.'

Dad clears his throat. 'Scarlett . . .'

'I said keep an open mind. Think about this. We could all get away from technology and devices. Danny could get away from his gaming.'

'Scarlett, my job is here . . .'

'Yes, but you could travel. Start your business again!

Amateur boxers aren't only in the city. I'm sure you'd find lots of raw talent out in the country.'

Dad rests his thick, broad hand on the table. 'Scarlett, we're not running from this.'

That's the thing about Dad. He never runs. Never lets me run, either.

'This isn't running. This is starting fresh.'

'Our community is here, champ.'

'No. What is here is a bunch of people who talk about me behind my back. And sometimes in front of it.'

His eyes soften. 'Did something happen at school today?'

'No, Dad. Something happens at school *every* day.'

I grab my printouts. Pass them to him. Middle of nowhere, fixer-upper cabins, with glorious views of the hinterlands from their sunny perches on top of mountain ranges.

'This one's got three bedrooms,' I say, showing him the pick of the bunch. 'A wood fire heater and stove, an outdoor bath and a stream running just below it. What's not to love?'

He studies it, but makes no comment.

'Okay, so it might be a little old and wooden looking, but you're good with your hands. And I'll help, I promise. Without school, I'd have time to learn so much. And Danny, he's almost as tall as you—he could help, instead of gaming on his laptop all the time.'

Dad glances briefly through the rest of the pictures before making a pile of them on the dining table. He pauses like he's trying to find the right words.

'Remember how Nikki said it was going to take you a bit of time to adjust?' he says.

'It's been seventeen months.'

'That's not very long.'

'It's too long.'

Dad closes his eyes and rests his forehead on his peaked fingers. 'You need to understand a couple things, champ.' He draws a big breath. 'Your treatments, they're ongoing. We're going to need specialist care for a little while yet.'

We won't. I will. And not for *a little while*. For years and years.

I collect my sketches and notes, my printouts of cosy wooden cabins. I bundle them together and push them aside. Along with all the hope they had lit up inside me.

'So it's a no?'

'It's a not yet.'

But I can see it inked in his eyes. No way this side of the century.

Nobody actually says the word 'no' to me anymore. They think I'm too fragile to hear it. Like a kid in preschool who only responds to positive reinforcement. 'It's not a good idea to stick your finger down that spider hole, Scarlett.' Instead of just saying, 'No, Scarlett, stop it.'

I push back my chair and leave my tea and biscuit untouched on the dining table. Leave my pile of useless research and sketches. I can't toss them out, toss my dreams out. He can do it. He already has anyway.

'Let's talk some more when Gran gets home,' he says.

That's how I know the idea is dead. Dad was my best shot. If he's not onboard, Gran will nail the idea shut for good. Even though Gran's the reason I need a mountain at all.

I grab my bag from the bottom of the staircase and head up to my room. It feels ten times heavier than it was on the bus. Why do they make you carry so much stuff to high school? Like it's not hard enough already. Different teachers for different classes, different groups of kids gawking at you, a million different books that need to be lugged around from one place to another in a bag as heavy as a load of cement.

I ditch my bag and shut my bedroom door. Lock it. My room sucks in the last of the day's light. The rest of the street can be drenched in shadow, but the sun saves its final blades of gold for me. As if my room is perched on its own little mountain. I slide my window open, pull in the flyscreen, lean my elbows on the windowsill and close my eyes. Where nobody can see me, I let the sun warm my face. Feel the tingle of light across my skin. Allow myself to bask in it.

When I open my eyes, the mountains are there, far across the city. Any mountain would do. I really wouldn't be fussy about which one.

I turn around so my back is facing the window and duck under the frame, reaching for the familiar downpipe grips. Unlike most of the houses in our street, our roof is tiled. And Anna taught me a couple of years ago that a tiled roof can be easily scaled. It's not slippery like metal roofs. So I climb the couple of rungs along the downpipe and pull myself up to the roofline. Belly first, I grab hold of the antennae anchor point, and I'm up. On top of the world. It's my secret escape—nobody knows about it. I can sit beside the antennae and watch over my world without anyone else sharing in it or ruining it.

The sun is kissing the ridgeline of the mountains. I know you're not meant to look directly at it, but it's hard to look away. I watch a spot just off to the left as the fiery ball is slowly swallowed up.

That's when the real show begins. I pull out my phone and take a few pictures as the blue ridgeline of the mountains makes a stark contrast against the dying yellow skyline. As I watch, the yellow gives way to burnt orange, umber and, finally, light blue.

Then I lie back against the cooling tiles, lace my fingers behind my head and watch the stars emerge from their shy places in the sky. Sometimes I feel like a star. Only safe to come out in the dark. I count the first brave ones to appear until I'm lost in their numbers, in their size, in their majesty. I used to love those first brave stars. The ones you point out, you count, you admire. Not anymore. If I were a star now, I'd choose to be one of the smallest. The kind that appears when there are enough to get lost in.

A scream wakes me. My body is covered in a slick of sweat. I'm wet all over. Even my hair is wet. The air is warm, but my body is cold and rippled in goosebumps.

Dad rushes in. 'It's okay,' he says.

He brings my bedside water to my lips. I drink it.

'Are you okay?'

I nod.

'It's just a bad dream,' he says. 'Come on.'

I do what I always do after the nightmares, and follow Dad next door to the spare bed, where he's slept ever since the accident.

Dad gives me a change of pyjamas and I wriggle under the fresh sheets, try to fall back to sleep. I feel the springs on the bed groan with his weight as he edges in on the other side, breathing deeply. We never talk about the dreams in the morning.

There are new footsteps now. The spare room door creaks open.

'Everything alright?' Gran's muffled voice.

A murmur from Dad. He sits up.

'She's asleep again,' Dad whispers. The bed squeaks as he gets out of it and treads quietly into the hallway where he eases the door half shut and plunges me into darkness.

'Nikki called me in yesterday,' he whispers to Gran.

I stiffen. They're the ones who make me go see the psychologist and now she's dobbing me in to Dad? I thought what we spoke about was meant to be private?

'She showed me Scarlett's art. How dark it is.'

Well, what do they expect? Rainbows and butterflies? I'm hardly in kindergarten. It turns out, there are no rainbows. The butterflies have tears in their wings. The windows in the houses are shattered, their fences are falling down. It happens. Brokenness and ugliness and ruined perfection. I won't pretend it doesn't.

'It's not normal, Ma. It chills me.' He lowers his voice until I have to strain to hear the words. 'She's dreaming of the flames . . . the burning . . .' Dad's voice breaks.

'Shh,' Gran says. 'Don't talk about it.'

This is the way it is with Gran. Let's pretend it never happened. Let's not speak of awful or ugly things. Scarlett should go back to dancing and wearing bright swimmers and doing everything she did before. There is no need to get away to a mountain.

All I want is for her to acknowledge it. Just once. To say, 'Scarlett, sweetie, I am so sorry that happened to you. I am so sorry I didn't do things differently.' Even though it wouldn't change what happened, it would be better if she could just stop pretending everything is okay.

It's not okay. Just like my dreams are not okay. But Dad's wrong about what's in them. I never dream of flames. Fire is just where oxygen and fuel collide to make light and heat. On its own, when it's calm and contained, fire isn't scary. It's only destruction that's scary.

I dream that I've woken from a long sleep and my face is perfect. I touch my cheeks, tracing the smooth unblemished skin along my jawline. Turn my head this way and that. I am me again. Beautiful. My face makes people smile. My blonde braids fall proudly over my shoulders. My lips are full and defined. A burst of joy breaks open in my chest. This is the girl I am. The true Scarlett. Pretty. Stunning. Gorgeous. My face lights up with a summery smile. But as my reflection smiles back, it cracks. Not the mirror, just my face. It cracks up like a smashed mug and the pretty mask crumbles off piece by piece.

Beneath it is an image too ghastly for human eyes.

That's when I wake. When I scream.

The nightmare is real. It's my forever.

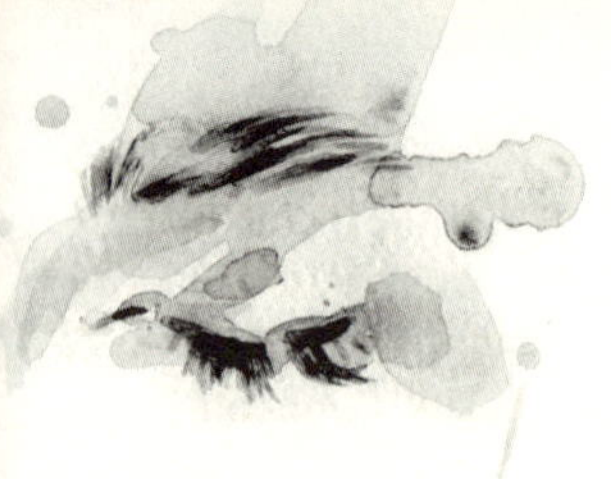

BEFORE

It's taking forever. The minutes tick by. My heart ticks with it, pumping at my nerves.

Half an hour until I'm up on stage before the judges.

I rehearse the dance in my head.

'I'm gonna be late for my game,' Danny moans from the back seat.

The afternoon traffic is thick and sluggish. Gran frowns at the car ahead.

'Get in the fast lane, Gran,' Danny says.

Gran looks at him through the rear-view mirror. 'You'll be walking if you keep that up. Scarlett's the one with the exam.'

'Always about Scarlett.'

'Is not,' I say.

'Listen, princess,' he says. 'There's more to life than dancing, okay?'

'Don't call me princess.'

'You are a princess.'

I spin around. 'Take that back.'

He raises his eyebrows and smirks. 'Are you gonna make me?'

'Take it back, Danny.'

'What are you gonna do if I don't? Pirouette on me?'

He laughs and looks out the window.

Without even thinking, my hand whips out. It lands on his thigh with a loud clap.

There's a red handprint on his skin.

His eyes go wide, then he catches my hand. Squeezes it in his. Squeezes until I wince. 'Don't you dare hit me. Ever. You spoilt little princess.'

'Cut it out, both of you,' Gran says sharply. 'You think fighting is going to get us there faster? I'll end up having an accident if you two don't stop distracting me.'

'Sorry,' I say to Gran.

Danny folds his arms and curses under his breath. Frowns out the window at the lines of thick traffic.

'Where are all these damn people going, anyway?' He slumps down low in the back seat. 'They're just clogging up the roads.'

'Probably doing the same as the rest of us,' Gran says, indicating left and squeezing us across to the next lane. 'Afternoon sports.'

When we pull up at the soccer fields, Danny's team is already playing.

'Great, I'm late.'

'Run,' Gran says.

Danny slams the door and sprints off to join his team.

I look at the clock on the dash. Like if I stare at it hard enough, I can stop the minutes turning.

'Fourteen minutes,' I say.

'I know, I know.'

Gran leaves the soccer fields in the rear-view mirror and turns back onto the main road. Back into the line of beetles crawling their slow way along.

'I'm going to miss it,' I say.

'No, you're not, beautiful girl.' Gran grips the steering wheel with both hands. Her knuckles are bony, almost translucent. 'I know how hard you've worked, and I'll get you there in time, one way or another.'

FOUR

If it's not one way, it's another. So many ways to be different. At school, everyone is very careful with their words. Cruel words aren't tolerated. If we didn't know this, we very quickly learnt, like Sebastian did earlier this year when he called me Scarface Claw. That one earned him a three day holiday from school. It earned me another nasty phrase for the nasty voice in my mind to whisper in the dark.

But there are lots of ways to be cruel if you really want to be, and some of those ways don't get you caught. And some days, people are cruel. Even the people you like. The ones you really like.

Today it's Oscar Jabore, his long hair pulled back in a loose ponytail, sitting in the back row of class, left-hand side, next to Byron. Maybe they're too busy talking to notice me slide into class, front row, right-hand side. Easy spot for a quick exit to lunch. Maybe they don't hear me enter. But I hear them.

'Top three hottest chicks in the grade,' Byron says. 'Go.'

I try to block it out. The names. The ratings. Why they do it.

Why it even matters.

Sometimes it feels like every girl is measured against a tree of perfection. How far from perfect does she fall? I guess I was close before, but now I fall below the roots.

'Summer Kowlinksi, number one,' Oscar says.

If it wasn't Oscar, maybe I wouldn't care so much. But I can't stop it mattering. Can't stop the ache throbbing in my stomach.

'Tyra Black and Anna Wang tied for second,' he says.

I've heard the boys do this countless times. Rating girls by numbers. Who's a ten out of ten? Who has the best body? The prettiest face? Who's the whole package?

I used to be on the 'best of' list. It's strange to think I'll never make that list again.

I battle through History with Mr Laforest. I try to focus on his words, but they flow around me, like I'm in a fast moving river. Nothing catches.

When the bell goes, I grab my bag and slip out of class. Straight to the toilet block.

I'm not sure why it bothers me so much that Oscar has Summer ranked as his number one. All I had was a tiny fourteen-year-old crush on him.

Maybe it's not Oscar's opinion I care about at all, but the ranking system itself. Why is being pretty so important? It's nice to be pretty, I know that much. I've been 'pretty'. And it's nice to be admired. After all, the world likes pretty things—Mrs Romano used to touch my hair every time we went to the fruit market, old Mr Sparks used to call out, 'Morning, pretty girl!' as I rode by on my way to school, kids' eyes used to follow me as I walked across the cafeteria. And when I danced, I was clapped and cheered. Even Byron and Oscar have it figured out. Pretty ranks above smart and rich and funny and sporty and, most definitely, above kindness.

You're born one way or another way. Some are pretty and some just aren't. It's luck. Nobody earns their looks. It's not like dancing, which takes hours of practise to get good at. It's not like boxing, which means sweating it out while the world is sleeping. Why do we make it matter so much?

On my tenth birthday, we were all seated around the dinner table. Gran, Dad, Danny and me. Gran was talking intensely, as she often does with a glass of wine in her hand, waving it around as she told Dad that people don't work hard enough anymore, that nobody does things thoroughly anymore. Danny and I were playing Scissors, Paper, Rock, our hands hidden beneath the table. Somehow, Gran started on about how she'd always wanted a girl.

'What I wouldn't have given for ribbons and curls and fairy dresses,' she said wistfully. 'Instead, I got dirty football gear and smelly socks.'

Gran had been robbed of her dreamed-of daughter. I'd heard about it since I was born. Of the little princess she'd wanted to dress in ball gowns, with all the lace and trimmings. How she'd wanted to braid her hair and press crystal pins in to fix it just so. I guess she wanted to share all the glamour from when she was runner-up for the Miss World beauty pageant in the old days.

But Gran got two boys. One a boxer, bent on punching people's faces. The other a rugby forward, who had enough injuries by the time he turned twenty to stop him playing.

Then I was born. I was the one who made it all up for her. The one who let her pin me into scratchy puffy dresses, curl my hair and spray it hard into place. Dad said no to beauty pageants. He wanted to train me to box. Gran said no to the boxing. Somehow I found dancing, and it fitted like I was born to it. All the grace of the beauty pageants with all the discipline and fitness of a competitive sport.

Gran loved to watch me dancing. 'Ballet is like watching an act of God—heavenly,' she'd say. But for Gran, ballet was only about the beauty—the outfits, the hair, the make-up, the perfect bodies.

Sitting around that dinner table for my tenth birthday, that was when I figured it out. How important it is to be beautiful. When Gran said, 'The only problem with having a girl is the risk of getting an ugly one.'

I looked up when she said it, but she didn't seem aware of me.

Dad cut in. 'Ma, surely you don't really think—'

'An ugly son is tolerable,' she went on, talking over Dad. 'Not that you're ugly, dear boy, but an unattractive boy might have the gift of the gab or be sporty or have some other redeeming quality. But an ugly daughter . . .' She raised her glass to her lips, tilted her head back and swallowed. 'I don't know that I would have coped. People always say it's okay, of course—what's on the inside and all that—but it never is really, is it?'

'Ma, that's actually very shallow. Looks do fade,' Dad said. 'And success isn't measured by appearances. Certainly not in boxing. And not in life either, I wouldn't think. Determination can get you a hell of a lot further than a pretty face.'

'Yes, I suppose that's true. But I've lived longer than you, dear boy, and what I've learnt is that, whether we like it or not, the world rotates around beauty. Beauty wins favours.' Her eyes met mine in that moment, and I saw their steely hardness mellow. 'Of course, sweetie, beauty is something you need never worry about. You have it in spades.'

Danny covered my rock with his paper. 'I win,' he said.

I remember sitting up a little straighter. Danny had beaten me in all three rounds, this was true. But I had beauty gifted to me. I would always have beauty.

I believed that too.

When I reach the toilet block, I push open the door and the cool air inside the bathroom is welcome against my warm face. My skin is extra reactive to the temperature now; the scars itch and burn on sweltering days, contract tightly on cold ones.

My cubicle is free. I lock the door, hang my bag on its hook, sit on the toilet lid and draw my legs up, hugging myself.

YESTERDAY MATTERED YESTERDAY

Deep breaths. Knead out the ache in my stomach.

My legs are unscarred. They still look normal. I can still stretch them behind my head the way I always could, but my arms struggle to reach back and catch them. Tight skin, lost muscle, still years of physio ahead.

Full-thickness burns to forty percent of her body. Torso, arms and face.

When doctors speak about you like that, you become a body. Not a person. How many parts damaged? The top half. How badly damaged? Three layers of skin deep.

But that's just the visible damage, isn't it? Those kinds of doctors are only trained to fix the physical things.

I run my hands over my legs. It's nice to still have smooth skin somewhere to remind me what that used to feel like everywhere. Back when I didn't appreciate it.

The bathroom door squeals open. Footsteps, laughter. Cubicle doors bang. Black shoes scuff alongside the bottom of my stall. I hold my breath.

'She won't be auditioning for the School Spectacular.' Pippi's voice. Distinctly high pitched. 'Maybe you have a shot at the lead this year.'

'Dancing's her thing. I bet she makes a comeback.' Anna. Talking about me. 'I'd rather that, than get the part.'

'Dancing's not her thing *anymore*. Not since she quit. Trust me, she won't be auditioning. You're in with a chance—you should go for it.'

I've never said I'm not going to audition for the School Spectacular. I even fleetingly considered the possibility of it. Standing in front of all the teachers and the entire school. Dancing as if nothing had changed. Of course, Pippi's right, and I'd never actually go for it. But I did let the idea drift through my mind from the safety of the moonlit roof the other night.

Toilets flush one after the other. Doors close, taps rush.

'Oscar's going for lead boy,' Pippi says. 'I heard him telling Byron. Scarlett will *not* be going. No way, no how. It would be cruel.'

'Cruel?'

'Well, yeah.' Pippi lowers her voice. 'Think about it. It must be extra devastating for her. To have been so pretty before . . . maybe it's karma?' Pippi almost sounds pleased about it. 'I mean, even her name: *Scar*lett. It's unfortunate.'

'That's actually really mean,' Anna says.

'I'm not trying to be mean, I'm just being honest.'

'Scarlett's still pretty,' Anna says. 'You just gotta squint.'

It's a knife to my chest. Short, sharp, in and out. It's the knife I didn't see coming.

The girls keep talking, but I don't hear anything else. My breaths are hard puffs, more punches than breaths. In, out, in, out. My arms tremble in their lock around my knees. I feel unsteady, like I'm going to topple off the toilet seat and spill out in front of these girls and their honest assessments of me. Spill out all my scars and blood and stitches and skin and pus. Dad tells me I'm a fighter. But I've seen enough boxing matches to know there are times the punches get too much. The boxer gets caught on the ropes. Not every fighter can win. And what good is a fist against cruel words, anyway? Not every fight happens in a ring.

I reach out a hand to steady myself against the cubicle wall.

The seat beneath me creaks. The voices stop.

No.

Stiff silence.

'I don't know,' Anna whispers.

More silence.

Scurrying feet, pushing doors, a blast of warm air.

No more words. No more feet. No more girls.

Anna has left me bleeding out on the floor. Not Pippi. Anna. Because Anna was trying to defend me. Anna meant it as kindness.

Anna is telling the truth.

I'm only pretty if you squint. She's trying to say what can't be said in the gentlest possible way: Scarlett is disfigured. Ugly. Offensive.

The words glare down at me from the toilet door.

YESTERDAY MATTERED YESTERDAY

No, it damn well doesn't. Yesterday matters *today*. It will matter *tomorrow*.

I no longer care who wrote the words or why. They're wrong. I grab a marker from my bag and beneath the lying words, I scrawl:

YESTERDAY MAKES TOMORROW. IT MATTERS. IT ALWAYS MATTERS.

I want no more yesterdays. No more todays. No more tomorrows.

It scares me how little I care. About dancing. About school. About next year. If death was a person, and he came to wake me in the depths of the night, I wouldn't scream. I wouldn't cry. I wouldn't plead. I would just let him wrap me up and take me away.

I have no will left to fight for life. I've spent it all already. And all I fought for was an *after* that isn't worth living. An *after* where I am ugly forever. At the bottom of everyone's list. The only thing I want right now is to escape my body, my face, my life.

I can't escape that, but I can escape school.

Dad says I should never run from anything. But he's never lived like this. He doesn't know what it's like to be me. Never in my life have I run from anything, but what if I need to run in order to survive? What if staying to face it is going to kill me?

Sorry, Dad. I'm giving myself permission to run.

After the end-of-lunch bell goes and the scurry of kids and bags and laughter dies down, I slip out of the toilet block. I make for the hedge line at the edge of the school yard. I can still run, and I'm fast. So I'm at that hedge and over it before anyone has noticed me.

No school bag, no laptop. Who needs them? The world I want doesn't consist of school or bags or technology.

I run until I'm breathless, until my face is pounding. Until I'm far enough away that I can sink down beside the low-slung concrete fence of a house and call Dad.

'I need you to pick me up. Are you at work?'

'You okay, champ?'

'Can you come? I'm at 29 Albert Street. Don't call the school.'

'Scarlett—'

'Please. Just come.'

I hang up, turn off my phone.

BEFORE

I turn on my phone.

4.25 pm.

The lights at the intersection grow larger as we near.

Green light turns to amber.

Amber hovers a moment.

Gran speeds up.

'Damn, red light camera.'

She slams the brakes on last minute.

An air horn blares behind us.

I turn around.

A monster of a truck in the rear window.

Skidding. Blasting.

Wheels locking.

Not slowing.

FIVE

Wheels slow to a stop at the kerb alongside me. It's Dad's dual cab. A jacked-up, monstrous, bright blue tank of a ute.

Dad, who never usually lets me run.

He gets out. Opens the passenger door. Scoops me up from the concrete like an injured animal and lifts me into the passenger seat. Clicks me in. Doesn't mention the tears soaking my face, or the snot running out my nose, or how stiff and trembly I am. He just grabs a couple of tissues and passes them to me. Then pulls a towel from the back seat and lays it over my legs. Like they did with the thermal blankets in the hospital after surgery.

We drive home in silence, past the school gate, which I refuse to look at. We stop at the set of lights just after the school and the fist in my stomach unclenches.

Is Dad angry? He's focused on the road, only casting a glance my way every so often. Then his hand is on my knee.

'Feeling any better, champ?'

'I'm not going back to school,' I say. My voice is alien, choked by tears. It sounds like it's coming from somewhere outside me.

'I can't do another minute of that hell.'

Dad stares straight ahead.

We drive the rest of the way home like this. Silent, except for the small hiccup noises of my sobbing. Still, except for the heaving of my body and his hand on my knee, leaving only to change gears.

By the time Dad crawls the ute into the garage, my body is racked with exhaustion.

He pulls on the handbrake. 'Let me tell you about the last fight I had.'

I close my eyes, breathe slowly out. I've heard this story a thousand times. Back in the glory days of his boxing career. Back when I was only just toddling around.

'Dad, I don't need you to pep talk me through this. I'm not going back. I can't.'

He ignores me, though, and he's got that far-away look in his eyes that tells me he's been transported back to his own *before*.

'That fight went the full twelve rounds. I was done after eleven. I mean, hell, I was fighting Maximus Mannis. It was a career ender. My eyes were so swollen from the hits, I could barely see. My eyebrow was split open, Scarlett, leaking blood all through my eyes and down my cheek. My ribs ached from the body strikes. The final round was going to be a knockout. Everyone knew it. Even I knew it.'

I listen numbly, waiting to hear what happened next. As if I don't already know.

'I was knocked out, of course. I don't remember when my team threw in the towel. I only saw that on the playback.'

'You were very lucky,' I say.

'I was. That final hit ended my career, but it could have ended my life.'

'I mean, you were lucky you had someone there who was willing to throw in the towel for you. Someone who could see you'd had enough.'

He stares at me a moment. Blinks.

'The point is, champ, I didn't run scared. It wasn't even about winning or losing. It was about looking my shaky fear in the eyeballs and saying, "I'm bigger than you. I'm not gonna be defeated by you." I was always gonna be defeated by Mannis. But I didn't have to be defeated by myself. I knew this much: when there's nothing left, you *can* still choose courage.'

I bite my bottom lip as I let those words sink in. I bite hard enough to dull the rage trembling to life in my gut.

'Do you think I haven't chosen courage?' My voice is small, but I manage to look him square in the eye.

He thinks for a moment, and that short pause tells me everything. 'You need to *keep* choosing courage.'

'Check out this face, Dad. I've worn it five hundred and twelve days now. I will wear it every single day for the rest of my life. I don't have any choice.'

'I know, champ. Your face is what the world sees. But it's not what you're made of.'

'That's crap. People show me every day that it *is* what I'm made of. After the accident, I thought I just had to fight for my life. So I fought. And I won. And what did I get for all my effort? The face of a monster.'

'You're no monster, Scarlett. Don't even speak like that.'

'Do you really think I haven't already tried courage, Dad? It's all used up. You went into that ring *once* and you tell it to me as one of the biggest moments in your life. But try doing that every single day. See how strong your courage is then.'

I open the passenger door of the dual cab.

'You know, it'd be nice to think I have people on *my* team who'd throw the towel in for me when I'm really struggling. Nobody ever says *I've* had enough.'

He says nothing back to me. Because there is nothing to say back. There are no answers.

I leave Dad sitting in silence in the car, clamber up the stairs to my room and blast my music.

Music is only sound. No pictures, no perfect faces, no perfect bodies. Music is about everything *imperfect*. Broken hearts and lives and people. It's the only thing that reminds me I am real.

I lie on my back and focus on my breathing. A warm, smooth trickle runs down my temples. Tears soak their familiar maps into the pillow either side of my head. There should be a limit to the number of tears a person can cry in a day, a week, a year.

Songs flick by on my playlist. *Song For Someone*, *The House That Built Me*, *Someone You Loved*, *I'm Still Breathing*, *Falling Up*, *Head Above Water.*

I listen to the words, absorbing everybody else's pain. I'm not the only one in the world who knows it. It's weirdly comforting.

My room turns golden with afternoon light, bright as a candle. My playlist repeats and my golden light fades with the sun.

There's a knock on my door. I turn the volume down,

but don't get up.

'Dinner's ready,' Danny says.

I couldn't eat if I wanted to. Can't face any of them with my swollen, miserable face. I have brought my family so much pain the last seventeen months. My misery is theirs too. Yet they expect me to keep powering through the days as though everything's okay. Gran hasn't even apologised. It wasn't exactly her fault. But man, I want somebody to blame. And she's the only one close enough. Not like I can punish the truck driver! If I had taken so much from someone, even if only by accident, I would damn well be apologising to that person.

I turn the music up again. *Before I Go*. I pump it so loud, the beat hums in my stomach. In the *before*, Danny would thump on our adjoining wall, pound on the door, text me something obnoxious. But these days, nobody tells me to turn my music down. Nobody tells me to do much of anything. Except Dad, today. Telling me to be brave.

Ha! Tried that, Dad. And guess what? Didn't fix it. Didn't make me pretty again. Didn't make me feel better.

Another bang on my door.

I turn the music down a notch.

'It's ready,' Danny says again.

'Not hungry.'

No response. No, 'Come on out, you spoilt little princess'.

He just twists my door handle. But I'm ahead of the game. It's locked.

'Gran, she won't come,' he calls out.

Then I hear him thumping down the stairs, two at a time.

There'll be a hushed conversation. 'She needs to eat,' from Dad. 'She'll eat when she's hungry,' from Gran. 'She needs to keep her strength up,' from Dad. 'She's not suffering from an eating disorder,' from Gran. I've heard it all before. They care so much.

I don't. I don't care about anything.

After the accident, everyone wanted to talk about my fight for survival. How scary that must have been.

It wasn't.

Fighting for your life is a moment by moment exercise. You don't think forward. You don't think about the rehab or the surgeries or the pain or the scars. You just think about the now, and sometimes not even that.

But the *after*? That's like the aftermath of a cyclone. When the excitement of the storm has passed, and all that's left is the damage. The recovery. Nothing to look forward to. Nothing to go back to.

My stomach meows, but I'm outside of my body now. Floating somewhere above my room, looking down at the girl sprawled on her back, arms and legs at weird angles by her side. The girl doesn't move. She looks peaceful. Her eyes are closed, but she doesn't sleep. She doesn't care to sleep or eat or do anything at all. She is so close to wanting nothing that she scares me.

I don't know how much longer she can travel like this.

A hard knock on the door re-joins me to her. Something sliding against the carpet.

I sit up, forcing myself to move. Telling myself how.

One leg off the bed, Scarlett. Now two. Sit up. Stand up.

Walk to the door, Scarlett.

At the base of the door, just inside my carpeted room, is a sheet of printer paper, face down.

I pick it up. My room is all but dark now, so I turn on the light. Squint against the harsh glare.

It's the printout of my cabin. The first one I showed Dad yesterday. My favourite wooden hut with the wood fire heater and stove. In the middle of blissful nowhere, on top of the world. I remember the sharp peaks of the blue-capped mountains from the pictures. The way it showed a layer of snow dusting the cabin in winter, purple wildflowers covering the hills in spring.

Beneath the picture, in Dad's tight, heavy writing, are the words:

You needed a mountain. ✓

You needed a forest full of trees. ✓

You needed a cabin to yourself. ✓

You needed a pack of dogs . . . will dingoes do the job? I reckon there'll be something prowling around.

I can't buy it for you, but it's up for holiday letting. How about we start with two weeks?

This is me throwing in your towel.

Love you, champ.

P.S. You'll want to get to bed early. We're leaving at first light.

AFTER

First, light. Bright, bursting, flowering light.
Then flames. Rushing, reaching.
Hot air, snatching at my throat.
Unclick belt. Struggle. Door stuck.
Flames closing in. Leaping, dancing, twisting.
Fists on glass. Banging.
Get out, get out, get out!
This is how I'll die.
Gran reaching. A man holding her back.
Gran fighting outside.
Me fighting inside.
No pain. Just heat, thick as soup.
Hammering heart. Smashing fists.
A woman screaming. Gran. Still reaching.
Get her out, get her out, get her out!
Voices.
Soft, loud, louder, more frantic.
People at the windows. Banging, smashing, yelling.

Sirens.

Fire growing. Leaping, dancing, twisting.

Amber, yellow, crimson, blue.

Burning rubber.

Hammer at my window. Burst of glass. Shower of glitter.

A snatch of blue sky.

'She's fading.'

'Get her out!'

Black sky.

Heat. Smoke. Heavy chest.

Screaming.

Blue sky.

Commanding voices.

'Get her out! She needs air!'

Black sky.

Tugging. Hands gripping, pulling.

Skin sliding down my arms.

Blue sky.

Cool rush of air.

Black sky.

'Stay with me, little girl. Stay with me. You've been in an accident, but you're gonna be okay. We'll get you all fixed up. Stay with me.'

Blue sky.

But my ballet exam . . .

Black sky.

Blue sky.

Black . . .

SIX

Black highway stretches ahead of us like a strap of liquorice. *Castle on the Hill* echoes through the loaded dual cab as we fly down the lonely highway in the early hours of what should be a work and school day.

Instead, we've cheated the rules of life. Bent them in our hands and twisted them into a new shape.

Who says we have to do what everyone else does? Go to work, go to school?

The next two weeks are about solitude and wilderness. I can pretend we never have to return to the real world. I can forget about Oscar and Pippi and even Anna. Anna didn't mean to be unkind and the further away we drive from all of them, the further away the pain feels.

I wind down my window, and Dad copies by winding down his. As he does one hundred down the highway, we let the air wash in and buffet our faces. Dad sings to the roaring wind, and I laugh. Then I do the same, letting the wind fill my cheeks and swallow my voice.

I clutch the map to our destination. Dad has the key. Every precious picture I could find of the cabin, I have printed and studied. Dad's phone's sat nav says it's four hours and forty-three minutes until our arrival, although we'll have to stop for lunch and breaks. I focus on the far-off mountains, trying to pick which one might be ours. Matilda Mountain. The pictures of it are rugged and glorious. Splintery trees and clear flowing streams and jagged peaks.

I am smiling. This in itself shouldn't be a big deal, except that I can't remember the last time I smiled. Something like sunshine is bubbling up inside me, spilling across my face.

I notice Dad looking across at me, one hand on the wheel, the ghost of a grin on his face.

'Happy, champ?'

I nod, turn my face into the breeze again.

Here in the ute with Dad, I don't need to look a certain way, or do a certain thing, or talk about anything I don't want to. I can just be. And we can run away, just for a little bit. Running's not so bad when you're running *to* something.

A pocked, weathered sign on the side of the road points up towards Matilda Mountain.

We turn left down a dirt road. Dad drops the ute into low gear as we begin to climb. The air is different here—cooler, sweeter. We travel slowly up the windy road, startling flocks of roadside galahs. The trees grow thicker and darker and older the higher we get.

'It's like a secret forest,' I whisper.

'All ours, champ. Just what the doctor ordered, huh?'

All ours. Just us.

The idea is thrilling.

The mountain track seems to climb forever, slow and twisty as we enter fog.

'The inside of a cloud,' Dad says, winding up our windows.

My ears pop with the pressure and misty rain dusts the windshield. The cloud is low, making everything dreary. Through the haze, a hand-painted sign declaring 'The Four Seasons' is nailed to a tree in a fork along the track. That's the name of our cabin, so Dad takes a sharp right.

I peer through the wooded track. A mob of kangaroos stand tall through the swirling mist, one ear cocked each, watching us approach before bounding away.

The trees grow sparse as we get higher, and the mist thins. Then, like something out of a movie, the fog is behind us, the wooded world grows clear, and I see it.

'There!'

I look from the crooked wooden cabin to the picture in my hand.

Identical. Perfect. Exactly what I ordered.

Dad slows the ute to a stop in front of the sagging wrap-around verandah, yanks on the handbrake and we both jump out. My skin is a prickle of goosebumps in the biting air and if the air were a colour, it would be green. It smells of moss and leaf litter and wet wood.

Gravel crunches underfoot and I take in a lungful of the crisp air.

I laugh, just once.

There is magic in newness. Places have power. And maybe in a different place, you can be a different somebody, with different worries and different cares.

Dad mounts the wooden stairs to the verandah, but I turn around to take in the view. We're on top of the world. The soupy layer of cloud we drove through on our way up runs like a ring of Saturn around the middle of our mountain. But beyond that, far beyond on the horizon, are velvety green hills shielding a sapphire stripe of ocean that cuts a straight line between heaven and earth.

'You coming?' Dad's poised with the key in the front door, looking at me.

There are no voices here but our own. No people but my own.

I follow Dad up the creaky stairs to the knotted oak door of the cabin. He tries the key in the lock. It's stiff, but he puts his shoulder into the door and heaves it open.

The air is chilly and musty. Cobwebs dust the corners of the large windows in the octagonal living room. Beneath the windows are low slung couches, flattened from age and use. A wood fire heater sits in the middle of the room, its flue disappearing through a hole in the ceiling. Dad did ask me on the way up if I'd be okay with the wood fire.

I want the wood fire. I chose the place with two wood fires. I need to show him it's not fire that scares me. No, Pippi, I am not the girl afraid of fire.

'Not exactly insulated, is it?' Dad says, checking out the ceiling. 'Reckon it'll get cold tonight.'

We walk around the living room, the floorboards groaning under our weight.

'Watch it.' Dad holds out a hand to stop me. 'Rotted planks. Why on earth would they rot?'

He looks up at the ceiling again. A coin of daylight shines down on us, reflecting off the tin roof.

'Is it too much to hope for no rain?' he says. 'These places are meant to be well kept.'

'Dad, it'll be fine,' I say. 'I just know it.'

And I do. I can't explain how I know we were meant to come here to this cabin on Matilda Mountain, but I do.

He locks eyes with me for a second. 'It will be, champ. I know it too.'

We walk past the slab kitchen with its quaint, wonky cupboard doors, and down the hall. Our footsteps are as loud as our voices are quiet.

Dad peers into the first room on the left.

'This must be the master suite, I guess,' he says.

It has a huge bay window looking out towards the distant strip of ocean. Sure, the bed's a little saggy in the middle. And a bare lightbulb hangs from a wire attached to the ceiling. But there are cute fake flowers on the bedside table and a bright green crocheted blanket that covers the bed and brushes the floor. This is exactly the right place. Not perfect, but safe. The kind of place that doesn't judge you back.

We check out the next two rooms and I pick the far bedroom, tucked away at the end of the hall. It has windows on two sides, so I can watch the forest trundling down to a stream far below from one, and the rolling hills from the other. It makes me feel a bit like that girl Heidi in the book, who lived with her grandfather on a mountain. It's chilly, but this room has a charm I can't resist with its wrought iron bed and sunshine yellow patchwork quilt. Yellow here seems like the colour of happiness. It is sunlight and wildflowers and butterflies.

I reach into my jacket pocket for my phone to take a picture, but then I remember where I left it. On my desk, in my room, in my old life. It will have text messages from Anna. Probably from Pippi too.

Pippi will only be worried that her mean words could get her suspended, but Anna will feel really bad about what she said. She didn't mean any harm by it. Which is why I texted her last thing before we left.

Scarlett

Heading off the grid for a while. Love you ♥♥♥

No, I don't want my phone. I don't need photos. Or the temptation to check out social media and the things of my old life.

I'm going back to basics. A pad of thick art paper. My set of twenty-four watercolour paints. Anything I want to remember from Matilda Mountain, I will paint. Like people used to do in the olden days. Before cameras captured every turn of your face and pictures of you were posted online every day for the world to see and criticise.

'Scarlett? Earth to Scarlett?'

I spin around. 'What?'

'Let's get unpacked.' Dad turns, then holds a hand out to the window closest to my bed. 'Where's that cold air coming from?

I do the same and a cool stream caresses my hand. The window behind the bed is the old-fashioned kind that slides up and down. Dad wrenches it up, and flakes of white paint flutter onto my lemon bedspread. He slams it shut again and the window panes rattle. But it's worse than before. The gap bigger, crooked, uneven.

'We'll sort that out later,' Dad says. 'Let's get our stuff.'

He leaves me in my room. I let out a contented sigh, stretch out my arms and do a slow, graceful pirouette. I don't care about a bit of cold air. I could live like this. Simply. By myself.

When I hear Dad opening the car door, I hurry after him, down the hallway and out the front door.

The verandah is baked golden in the last light of the afternoon and it makes me wonder if whoever built the cabin picked this spot to catch the last rays of the day. I tilt back my head and let the dying afternoon light leak into my face. I can only risk this when the sun's at its weakest. Just rising, just setting, it doesn't inflame my skin. But damn it feels good.

'Wait, I promised Gran a photo,' Dad says. He pulls out his phone.

'Not of me.' I shrink back against the house.

'Not even one, to remember this?'

'No time, Dad. You said yourself, we need to get unpacked before dark.'

I run down the steps before he can argue and busy myself hauling bags out of the back of the ute. I don't want any more photos. What's the point? I'll never be brave enough to look at them. The mirror's bad enough.

We hear it through the dark. A whooshing noise. A slam against the cabin wall. I jump.

'What was that?'

Dad is next to me on the lounge. He puts his plate of half-eaten pizza on the floor. The wood fire rages in the middle of the room, heating the lounge room and adding to the amber tinge of the dim lightbulbs hanging from their wires in the ceiling.

Another slam. Followed by a roar.

'Wind,' Dad says, standing up.

But wind is too soft a word for what's hitting the house.

'A squall's blowing in.'

Now a bang. Then a skittering across the tin roof. Leaves maybe, or twigs.

'What's a squall?'

'A localised storm. It's okay.'

The logs burn on in the wood heater, unconcerned. But I'm concerned. I brace as the next gust hits the house. Stronger this time, cool air rushing through the crevices in the cabin walls and sending a chill through my stomach.

Dad goes for the front door.

There's another gust, and a ghostly wailing as the wind bursts in through the hole in the ceiling.

'Geez,' Dad says.

He opens the oak door, but it's blown clear from his grip by the next burst of wind and slams hard against the timber panelling. Leaves whip inside. Dad holds the door open with his back.

'I better move the ute.'

And with that, he wrestles the door shut behind him.

'Dad, wait!'

He doesn't hear me.

I run to Dad's bedroom, which faces the ute, turn the light on and kneel on his bed. I peel back the sheer curtains to watch.

Twin beams of light pierce the night as the ute engine growls to life.

A tapping noise begins on the roof. First a few light taps, then heavier, louder. The wind picks up. It's no longer slamming into the house, but howling around it. A ferocious sound, like a beast trying to prise the tin roof from the cabin with gnarled fingers, bolt by bolt. Icy air shoots through the cracks around Dad's window frame.

A flash of light gives a skeletal snapshot of the sharp trees. In the night, they are all sticks and angles and jagged branches. Thunder growls.

The ute crawls forward. Dad's lights cut a path through the razor blades of rain. It drums on the roof so hard I can feel the vibrations in my teeth. Dad stops beneath a thick gum tree.

One that looks sturdy enough to stand through a storm.

A white hot bolt of lightning spears into the earth and thunder cracks with fury. It doesn't care how fragile I am. It doesn't care what's happened to me or why. The storm refuses to tread carefully. It wants to be seen. To be heard. To be known. And it makes me feel electric.

A thud, a crash, a screech.

The lightbulb hanging above me blinks off.

The world is dark.

AFTER

The world is dark then light. I swing like a jack-o-lantern between the two.

Dark is nicer, cooler.

I'm tired. So tired. My eyes are heavy, so I let them stay shut.

Whispers.

Voices.

They echo through my brain.

Day or night, awake or asleep, I don't know. I don't care.

Time is nothing.

Beep of machines.

Smell of antiseptic.

Multi-coloured dreams . . . big rainbow lollipops and sour strips, bubble-gum and mints, hot pink cupcakes, marshmallows and fruit jellies.

Dancing. Someone is dancing. Someone is meant to dance. Someone, somewhere, ballet.

Through the darkness, noises. Muffled, mixed.

A soft, high voice. A low, deep one. A cold, clinical one.

The sounds join into focus.

'Full-thickness . . . layers . . . skin . . . surgery.'

A whimper.

'She was so beautiful.'

A sob.

The words are far away, in the distance. Not even real.

'Love you, champ.' The low, deep voice is familiar. There's a comforting rhythm to it.

Warmth on my forehead.

Beep, beep, beep.

'She's coming round.' No comfort in this voice.

'Can she hear us?' The higher, softer one.

Dry. My mouth. So dry.

Something awful covering me. A fog, a web, a cage.

I lift my hand. Too heavy. Metal weights in my arms, my legs.

I open my eyes. Squint.

Blazing light. Too bright.

A moan.

Shut my eyes. Back to the dark. The cool.

'She's awake.'

'Welcome back, Scarlett.' The cold voice.

'Hello, sweetheart.' The soft, high voice.

'Gran?' But there's no sound from my mouth. Just air.

'Sweetheart, we're here.'

Pressure on my hand. Pain in my hand.

I grimace.

Open my eyes. Squint against the glare.

Lights dim. Shapes slide into view.

White sheets. White faces. White bandages.

A world of white. A world of pain.

I look down. I'm covered. Wrapped like a fly in a gauzy web.

Words that won't form.

A hand resting on my shoulder. Warm and gentle and large.

'You're gonna be okay, champ.'

I look up at the voice. Dad. His mouth smiles, but his eyes don't. His eyes are wet. I look at Gran. Her eyes don't smile either. It's like someone has turned off their lights.

SEVEN

Dad turns off the lights on the ute. He opens the driver's door and steps out before a gust of wind slams it shut. Then, shielding his face with one arm, he doubles over and bolts for the house.

Behind me, the hallway is a faint orange glow. I run down it to meet him, wrenching open the front door.

A burst of cold air rushes in. Dad heaves the door shut behind him, leans back against it. Firelight flickers warped shadows across his face. His dark curls are wet and plastered to his forehead, running rivers into his eyebrows.

'The thing about mountaintops,' he says, breathing heavily, 'is the wind. And rain. And storms. They don't mention that in the ads, huh?' But Dad's grinning as he says it. 'If it's a wild west adventure you wanted, champ, looks like it's the wild west you're gonna get.'

In answer, thunder cracks above us and the floorboards tremble.

Dad locks the door, peels off his jacket. He hangs it along the lounge near the fire.

'Let's get some light happening.'

I follow him to the kitchen and we rummage for a torch, which we use to find a stash of candles hidden in the cupboard.

We line the candles up on the kitchen bench, before Dad lights them, one by one, with a box of matches. He doesn't ask me to help him. I don't offer. It goes unspoken. But I'm not scared.

As Dad positions the candles around the room, I find a saucepan to catch the rain dripping through the hole in the roof and onto the living room floor. Then we sit back to survey our work.

Water pings into the saucepan and candlelight flickers around the cabin walls. Stretched skinny flames, short fat flames, wobbly jagged flames.

'Look, they're dancing,' I say.

See, Pippi? I'm not afraid of fire.

'Ballerina candles,' Dad says.

By the time he walks me to my room with the torch, the storm has passed, leaving only the wind in its wake. It moans through the gap in my bedroom window like a ghost.

'Damn, I meant to fix that,' Dad says.

I pull back my bedspread, but it's heavy.

'It's wet.'

Dad shines the beam of light over my happy yellow quilt. The entire thing is saturated.

The other room is cold and stark by torchlight. Small coffin-like walls house one narrow iron bed. The kind that might have lived in an orphanage a hundred years ago. But it has a thick patchwork quilt. And it's dry.

‘This’ll do,’ I say, pulling back the blankets and climbing into the bed.

‘I’m just in the other room,’ Dad says.

That’s when I realise he’s not next door. He has slept in the spare room next to mine every night in the *after*. One thin gyprock wall dividing us.

Dad pulls the covers over me in the bed, like he used to do when I was five. Then he kisses me gently on the forehead. He never says ‘sweet dreams’ anymore. We don’t kid ourselves. He just says, ‘Love you, champ. I’m here if you need me.’ Then he pads back down the hall.

I lie on my back in the dark, listening to leaves trotting across the tin roof. I hear Dad’s bed creak with his weight. A cough, a mutter. I try to make out the shapes around me in this closet-sized room, but my eyes are too heavy to care, so I let them drop.

A scream wakes me.

I bolt upright in bed. A hard, mean-looking bed.

Walls press in on me.

My breaths are heavy gasps.

My chest wet, slippery. Hair, drenched.

A silhouette hovers over me.

Another scream.

Mine. Animalistic. Blood curdling.

‘It’s me, it’s Dad.’

My breaths are raspy in the dark, my throat sore.

'We're in the cabin. On your mountain. You're safe.'

I wipe the cold sweat from above my eyebrows. Dad edges down on the bed, strokes my wet hair.

'Nightmares?'

I nod. But it's not nightmares. It's one. One nightmare. The one I have over and over.

My heart is still galloping and the same sick feeling settles into my chest when I remember the face is real. All of this, real.

'Why don't you have a drink?' Dad picks up my glass from the bedside table, squints at it to check there's water in there, then hands it to me.

I press the cool glass against my lips and drink.

Then I follow Dad across the hallway, still glowing from the fire, and he pulls back the blankets for me on the disused side of his bed. He never makes me feel bad about this. Never mentions the fact that fourteen-year-old girls should be sleeping in their own beds. Just lets me climb in like I'm a toddler, and we both pretend it's normal.

Dad gets into the bed and my heart slows down. I haven't figured out if it's the smell of him that has this effect on me, or just his presence, but it has worked like magic every night since the accident. I listen as his breaths grow deep and slow. From the firelight in the hall, I can see the light stubble on his face, flecked grey. The scar on his right cheekbone from that fight with Maximus Mannis. The scar splitting his eyebrow in half from the fight with Mick Lee. Dad's only ever been proud of his scars, never ashamed. *These remind me of the times life tried to beat me and lost*, he says. Why can't I feel the same way about mine? Why do my scars have to be so damn ugly?

Dad begins his light snore, and I close my eyes. Anna hates it when her dad snores—she says she wants to peg a shoe at him—but not me. Not ever. A dingo howls far away, but with Dad beside me, nothing from the outside can get in to hurt me. Not dingoes or storms or fires or people. It's the only place I'm safe.

I fall back asleep, but I don't dream about my face. I don't wake screaming again. I just sleep and sleep and sleep.

When I wake, a stream of light is burning my eyes and I'm alone in Dad's bed. I have no idea what time it is, so I reach across and swipe open the sheer curtains.

A deep blue, cloudless sky waits for me. As if we'd only imagined last night's storm.

Then I hear Dad's voice. His raised voice.

'Look, I barely slept a wink last night from the wind and the rain and the leaks and the cold, and we've lost all power. The roof is leaking, one of the beds got drenched in the storm, I thought my ute was going to be written off, and, to be brutally honest, the cabin's not really fit for human habitation.'

I sit upright.

'I want one of two things: either you send a repair guy out here today to restore power and fix the leak in the roof, or you give me a full refund for the two weeks and we'll be gone by sundown.'

Gone?

I leap out of bed and pad down the hallway to where Dad is pacing in the living room.

His eyes catch mine, and I shake my head furiously.

'Yes, I need the power back on by tonight. Thank you.'

Dad ends the call.

'We've had one night here! One night out of—'

He holds up a hand.

'We're not leaving. Not yet, anyway. We paid good money for this cabin. But I'd like the elements to remain outside, not inside. Power should be back on today, but we need to fix this place up.'

'It is a bit of a fixer-upper,' I grin. 'Aren't we all, though?'

'I'd prefer it to be liveable.'

I turn to the window that showcases the rolling green hills. 'But the views. Oh Dad, I'd live with a cold leaky bedroom forever for views like this!'

'Let me just remind you where you *didn't* sleep last night.'

After breakfast, I dress while Dad showers. The day already feels warm, so I go for my denim shorts and a loose-fitting, long-sleeved white shirt.

By the time Dad's ready, I'm outside, hat on, gloves on. The sun is warm on my back as I stretch my arms.

'Alright, fists up, champ.' Dad holds the red mitts up below his chin. My target pads. 'Let's show Matilda Mountain and all who dwell on her what you've got.'

I grit my teeth, fists raised to my eyes, elbows tucked in to protect my ribs.

Dad does the usual warm-up routine and then we work on combinations. Jab, cross, hook, uppercut, uppercut. He shadows me with his mitts and swats my fists away as they come at him, until I'm panting and hot. My arms quickly grow weak. They have maybe half the strength they used to have. They may not ever get stronger. And dancers . . . dancers need strong arms.

'Harder, champ. You can go harder than that.'

I punch at the mitts. Over and over I punch them, until my punches lose power and my arms ache and all I can do is kiss the mitts with my fists.

Finally, my gloves hang limp and wobbly down by my sides. I've reached my limit.

'Come on, one more.'

'I can't.'

'You can. One more.'

I raise my fists and the gloves feel like lead. I push for one final combination into his mitts, then collapse in a heap on the ground, arms stretched out either side.

'I'm finished,' I say, closing my eyes against the glare of the sun.

Dad slips off the mitts then crouches beside me to unstrap my gloves. 'You did good today. You're really getting stronger, huh?'

'Doesn't feel like it,' I groan.

'Hey, a year ago you could barely lift your arms. One punch at a time.'

I pull myself up off the ground, and nod. 'One day at a time.'

We get to work on the cabin. I scrunch strips of newspaper into tight little balls and Dad stuffs them into the crevices between the window frames in the living room. There's not much we can do about the leak in the roof, but I help Dad strip my bed and we hang the sheets and blankets over the verandah railing to dry. They buffet in the light breeze, like flags full of sunshine.

I follow Dad round the side of the house to where the wood pile is. Cylinders of wood have been sliced from fallen tree trunks and are stacked neatly on their side in rows beneath the verandah. Some are only the width of my arm, but others are thick and ringed. I run my finger down the rough surface of one of the big cuts.

'I wonder why the rings are different colours,' I say.

'Depends when the wood was growing.' Dad picks up a block splitter axe that's lying next to the pile. 'From what I remember, the lighter rings are the ones that grew in spring. Darker rings in autumn. The older the tree, the more rings.'

'This ring's black,' I say. 'This one in the middle.'

Dad examines the cross section of the log. 'So it is. I guess trees are like the rest of us—they have tough seasons. Maybe that tree survived a fire too, champ.'

Dad reaches for a cylinder of wood from the top of the pile, rests it on the base of a tree trunk full of axe marks.

'Maybe just leave this one,' I say, patting the chalky bark. 'Don't cut it up. Nobody needs to be burnt twice.'

Dad looks at me. 'I won't touch that one. You have my word.'

Then he raises the axe high over his shoulder and lets it thud heavily into the block of wood on the splitter. Dad hacks at it until the wood splits a star in its middle, then breaks into three triangular pieces.

He grabs the next piece and raises the axe.

'I might go gather some kindling,' I say.

I leave Dad focused on his job and start gathering sticks in my arms. There are plenty around after last night's storm, but I'm overcome by wanderlust. Birds trill from the high-up spindly branches of she-oaks and I can just make out the sound of trickling water in the distance. Must be the stream I saw from my bedroom window.

I dump my pile of sticks under the verandah where they'll stay dry and follow the music of the stream. A lot of my parts got damaged in the fire, but my ears weren't one of them. The noises out here are quiet. Instead of the loud, bossy voices at school, I have the crunch of leaves underfoot, the slither of a lizard beneath a stand of bracken, the call and answer of birds.

I wander downhill, through scrubby bush grass, between clumps of thick-trunked gum trees and tall-peaked she-oaks. The gurgle of water gets louder. I think of air, fire, water, earth. Ancient elements that have kept humans alive for thousands of years. But also sometimes killed them. Air can become toxic, fire can burn, water can drown, earth can bury.

Not today, though.

The deep blue sky pours down on me, and the gargle of the stream gets closer, till I can hear the rush over pebbles and the gush over ledges.

The edge of the bank is bathed in golden light. A willow tree to my left dips her bright leaves into the stream, and water pours over a log that's fallen across the creek, cascading clear and clean down into the valley. Away to some pool I'll never see the bottom of.

A branch cracks behind me. I turn around. No-one there.

My spine prickles. The feeling of eyes. Like I'm being watched.

A flicker of movement on the far side of the stream.

That's when I see her. On the opposite bank, hiding between the tall reeds. Still as a painting, white spots on her rear, ears parted sideways, big wide eyes fixed on me. We lock eyes, neither of us daring to move.

I've never seen a deer in the wild. I don't want her to go. I want to tell her it's okay, I won't hurt her. But a bird swoops out of a tree, and the deer startles. She keeps her eyes on me as she leaps, graceful and lithe, before prancing off into the thicker woods.

I smile at the dance of my sweet wild deer. Not the trapped kind you see in zoos, the free kind performing for no-one.

Maybe I can dance too, if it's just for me?

I've tried so hard to forget my routines. The music, the steps, the way it feels to stretch my arms high above my head.

Like everything else I've wanted to forget though, my memory clings on.

I lift my arms out to either side of my body, let them float gently back down. The muscles are tighter, weaker, smaller. They hurt. But they've not forgotten how to move.

I pull up first one leg to stretch it against my ear, then the other. I lean forward, pointing one leg out behind me, arms outstretched and trembling, like a scared little bird. My standing leg wobbles beneath me, but I hold steady, dip further forward.

I lower my leg back to first position and stand tall again, lifting my arms into first, then second. I reach above my head, as close as I can get to fifth position. My muscles burn, but I hold the pose before letting them rest back down in brasbas.

The movements are both foreign and familiar. Like reading an old book from when I was small.

I pirouette on the spot. First once, then twice, three times.

I stop, and look for my deer, but, of course, she's not watching. She's long gone. So I do a small leap in her honour, my legs splitting apart in the air. Then I spin to the earth, tucking myself up small. Back to the start of the routine for *Bird Set Free*.

In my head, the music plays. Gently and softly at first, as I unfurl from my position and rise, before falling dramatically back to the ground, my hands splayed out on the earth in front of me.

Then I'm up and jumping, pointing my toes to the dirt. I pirouette again, more confidently this time, face tilted to the sky.

I move through the piece, remembering the steps, blocking out the thought of the judges who would see me now if I were to go back. Judges who have known me since I was in Twinkle Toes. But there are no judges here. No ballet exams. Nobody at all.

I am dancing. That's what matters. I haven't danced more than a step since the accident. I envisage a crowd of animals watching me . . . birds in the branches, kangaroos on the banks of the stream, maybe a koala gnawing on a gum leaf up high. What do they think of this human girl dancing in the bush?

A clapping noise stops me mid-step.

I whip around to face the inky trunks of giant gum trees.

Nothing. Silly.

But there it is again. Another clapping noise, higher up.

I squint into the branches of the willow tree bending its fluorescent leaves into the stream beside me, but sunlight is bursting through the canopy and all I see is something stripy.

It jumps down lithely. Lands on hands and knees, and springs straight up.

'Hey, you're good.'

It's a boy. Broad freckled face, ears that stick out either side and a mop of dark dreadlocked hair.

A human. On my mountain. And by the look of him, a human roughly my age, which means there will be more. Humans my age aren't allowed to roam mountains alone.

All thoughts and words vanish from my mind. Like I no longer have any language. The blood pumping through my body slithers from my head and vital organs down to my feet.

The boy doesn't seem to notice any of this. He just dusts a hand on his grubby knee and extends it.

'Eamon Boyce. From down the hill.'

I stare at his hand like I don't know what to do with it. I don't take it or shake it, so after a little while, he drops it.

'You're on private property.' My voice is off kilter, but how dare he be on my mountain?

The boy shrugs. 'It's all pretty private, far as I can tell.'

He studies my face, so I look down at the chipped gum leaves crunched beneath my joggers. With his eyes roaming my scars, I've lost all courage. I know what he sees.

'You staying in the cabin?' he says. 'Nice bit of rain we had last night, hey.'

'It wasn't nice, actually,' I snap. 'We lost our power.'

'Yeah, that happens. It comes back on eventually.'

I don't want to know how he knows this. Or why he's here.

I'm not interested in making new friends. Or even keeping old ones. Not interested in people full stop.

'So you're a dancer?' he says. 'I like that spin thing you did.'

'You shouldn't be spying on people.'

'I wasn't spying. I was just sitting in my usual spot waiting for a bite, and you came down and did that little dance.'

'I did *not* come down here to do a little dance.'

'Hey, chill. I didn't mean it in a bad way. Dancing's nice. It's kinda . . . beautiful.'

There's a short sharp pain in my heart. How *dare* he?

I turn from the boy and, with legs that still work, I run. I am the deer. Not as pretty, but every bit as quick.

AFTER

'Quick.' A voice from far away. 'We need a vein.'

'I can't find one. She's too swollen.'

'The incisions along her arms should release the pressure. Here, let me try. We need to get the IV line in.'

On fire. My body is on fire.

They have cut away my dead skin, these doctors.

Sliced open my swollen arms.

Wrapped me in skin.

Plastic skin and donor skin and strips of my own skin, stretched out thin.

Skin to cover what was lost.

Still, my body burns. It doesn't like the new skin.

Swelling.

Hot.

Infected.

Rejected.

A heart monitor beeps. My heart is dancing.

Dancing to a fast irregular beat.

It won't slow down.

EIGHT

I don't slow down. I run and I run and I run.

I thought I could escape the world, but really, the whole idea of a cabin on a mountain sucked. Pretending I'd never have to see anyone again. People find you, don't they? No matter where you run, there's always someone there to hunt you down. Stare at you. Talk about the way you look, the way you dance. The deer was right to bolt.

My legs ache from running uphill, but I push on. The pain is good. I want it to swallow me up. With each breath I drag into my lungs, the tears on my cheeks sting a little colder. I gasp. Up I run, pushing my body, legs quivering now, but still I push.

If I was made with this face, I think I could accept it. But this isn't me. It's the face of a stranger and I want it to go away. I want to put one of those magic filters on that blend my face back to normal. That's what my plastic surgeon was meant to do. Step by slow step. Surgery by painful surgery.

'Pain is beauty,' she'd said to me with a smile.

But is it meant to hurt this much to look pretty? How much

pain does it cost to become beautiful?

When we first met the plastic surgeon, I thought she was going to cut me up and stitch me back together like I was before. Plastic surgeons make famous people beautiful, don't they? Give them prettier noses and cheeks and smiles and teeth and anything else they ask for. I know, I looked it up. Plastic surgeons can even sew dimples into your face if you want them badly enough. So I thought the job of the plastic surgeon was to make me more beautiful. But I was wrong. It was to make me less ugly. And it's not even working. Not fast enough, not perfect enough. Nowhere near. Too many thick scars and lumpy red bits.

Gran tells me it's okay—there's make-up, lots of make-up. But she knows as well as I do that no amount of make-up can make me beautiful. And part of me, deep down, wishes I had stabbed her in the thigh with my fork when she talked about ugly girls over the dinner table on my tenth birthday. She was so sure that I was safely beautiful. Sure enough to tell me what she really thought. And her thoughts were uglier than any person I've ever met. I wonder how she feels now that she belongs to an ugly girl?

The cabin comes into sight, a small oblong against a line of splintery trees. A squat, dark box. A leaky, powerless, cold, wind-ridden old thing. No magic in it. No magic in Matilda Mountain. Magic is for people like Harry Potter, who escape to wizard schools to cast spells and get rid of evil ugly things. When you *are* the ugly thing, there's no escaping yourself. No way to outrun it.

Dad's stacking wood in a pile. He looks up as I stagger past him and up the steps of the verandah into the cabin. I burst through the door and the cool air inside swamps me.

'Scarlett?'

Don't. Don't call me that. *Scar*lett. Unfortunate name.

I breathe in gasps, hiccups—half sobs, half desperate grabs for air. I bolt down the hallway, into my room and yank my suitcase out from under my bed. Jackets off hangars in the wardrobe. Into the suitcase. T-shirts out of drawers. Dump them on top. My paints, my thick pad of paper, unused. It all flies in to create a messy heap.

It's over before it even began. My escape.

'What are you doing?'

I startle at the voice in the doorway, but keep going. My book, my shoes, my beanie. All of it making a huge mound in my case.

I flip the lid shut and try to zip it up, but things aren't folded neatly, so the lid doesn't close. I throw my weight onto it, zipping down one side, jamming things in, shaking, crying.

The zip won't move.

The bag won't shut.

The people won't go.

The words won't stop.

Beautiful. Ugly. Pretty. What do those pathetic words even mean?

'Champ, what are you doing?'

I'm crying, Dad. Crying because people care so much about beauty. Here on a mountain, away from other people's eyes and thoughts, my looks should mean nothing. No-one to see my face. No-one to judge whether it's pretty or ugly. Who is being beautiful even for? Everyone else?

That damn boy has ruined it. He's ruined it all. I wasn't

dancing for *him*. I was dancing for me. *Just* me. How dare he tell me it was beautiful? I didn't want his thoughts. He shouldn't even *be* on my mountain. I don't give a toss what he thinks about my dancing. Or what he thinks is beautiful. I'm here for me. Only me.

Why does an ugly girl even need to redeem herself? A pretty girl is worth something in the eyes of the world, but if you're not pretty, Gran says you'd better be sporty or musical or artistic or smart or something. Do I need to become the perfect dancer now to make up for my scars? Because people expect dancing to be beautiful? Byron Maroni doesn't need to be extraordinary because of his dog attack scars. Nobody expects a boy to be beautiful. That's a girl's job.

Dad picks me up off the suitcase and holds me in his tattoo-sleeved arms, clutching my hair.

'Tell me,' he says in my ear. 'Tell me what's going on.'

'We. Need. To. Leave.' Between sobs.

'Why, what's happened?'

I shake my head. He lowers us to the bare mattress, which sags beneath our weight.

'You can tell me anything, you know that.'

I take a deep breath.

'A boy.'

'A boy?'

I half-laugh, half-sob at how ridiculous that sounds.

'I met a boy down by the river.'

Dad turns to me. 'Did he do something to you?'

'No, Dad. Nothing like that.'

'What then? Who is this kid?'

'How the hell should I know?' I wipe my nose with the back of my hand. 'It's just . . . people are everywhere. Even up here.'

'You're upset because you ran into someone, is that it?'

I nod quietly, tears sliding down my cheeks.

'Champ, you've got to exist in a world of people.'

'Not up here I don't. Not on *my* mountain.'

Then I'm crying again, great heaving sobs. Dad's arm remains firmly round my shoulder.

'Scarlett, you can't run away from all of civilisation. You deserve to belong to it. The world of people.'

I shake my head.

'I don't want to.' My voice is small. 'I wanted to be alone. Just us. But everything I want . . . it just seems to . . . crumble.'

'Oh, champ.' Dad pulls me closer. 'It's not like that.'

'It is. It's useless.'

'It's not useless. We're alone now, aren't we?'

Dad drags my bedroom window up, cups his hands round his mouth and, as loudly as he can, he yells, 'Cooooooooooeeeeeeee!'

His voice echoes back at us and I laugh, sniffing back my tears.

'Alone, see?'

I nod.

'Maybe that boy was a local from somewhere. What was he doing down there?'

I shrug. 'He said something about fishing, but I'm not sure.'

'Did he say anything to upset you?'

I shake my head.

'You'd tell me if he did?'

Dad takes his arm from my shoulder and rolls up his sleeve, so all his tattoos are showing. I know he could cuff any guy who spoke badly to me. I hope he wouldn't, but he could. In between tattoos of boxing gloves and dates are symbols I don't understand. There's also my face and Danny's as toddlers, our names and birthdays, a pair of wedding rings.

'Tattoos tell stories—that's why I got them. My story on my body. Like these rings, they're about your mother. Love can die in lots of ways, but I think ours died the best way. Without growing old or bitter.'

He rarely speaks to me about his relationship with Mum. We talk about her as my mum, of course, but not really about their love. I've always felt like it makes him sad. Both because she died when I was little, and because we never got to be a regular family like everyone else in our neatly primped street of perfect hedges and fences. Instead of a mum, I got a gran. And Gran has done so much more than a gran should ever have to do. Without complaining too. But I wonder if Dad wishes he could talk about Mum more. Without remembering the cancer and all the awful bits at the end.

'You don't remember her, do you?'

I remember her sleeping in a shiny wooden box. My small fingers pressed against her cold forehead.

'Not much.'

'That's why I got her face put here, on my heart. But you know, champ, if tattoos tell stories, scars tell even better ones. This one here,' he touches the line that splits the far edge of his eyebrow down the middle like a fork of lightning, 'this is the story of when

I beat Mick Lee in the eleventh round by technical knockout. And this one,' he traces his thick finger down my cheek, 'this marks the day my girl became a warrior.'

I flinch from his touch. I don't like people touching my skin anymore, not even the people I love.

'It could have gone either way for you, champ. I'm not sure how well you understand that, but for a while there . . .' He clears his throat. 'But you fought. Like I *knew* you would. You went the full twelve rounds and then some. You're still fighting. You think I don't see it.'

'You don't need to see it.'

'I see it every day. I see it in the slow way you pack your bag for school. I see it in your locked bedroom door and your blasting music and the way you don't dance anymore. I see it in every single tear you cry. And it breaks me, it damn well *breaks* me. But then I think of the time I got matched with Vince Croft. Vince was heavier, hadn't lost a single match in his career, five years younger. But I strapped up anyway. I met him in the ring. You and me, champ, we're made of the same stuff.'

I smile wryly. 'And what stuff is that?'

'Grit. Scars. This face tells me my girl is a survivor. Life tried to break you and it couldn't.' He wraps his arm around my shoulder again and squeezes me. 'I'm that proud to call you mine. And you know that boy? He's not even worth a single one of your tears. I bet you never see him again.'

Dad fixes my bedroom window firmly shut just as a faint growling noise starts up in the distance. The growl gets steadily louder. A car engine.

'Finally,' Dad says, heading down the hall to the verandah. 'The power guy.'

'He won't come inside, will he?'

'Doubt it, champ. But we want our power on by tonight.'

I stay in my bedroom and watch through a crack in the curtains as a jacked-up four-wheel drive lumbers up to the house and stops. Strapped to the roof racks is a ladder.

A tall older man in a navy button-up shirt, grey hair sticking out at weird angles from his head, gets out of the car holding a metal box in one hand. He smiles at Dad, and his face breaks into brackets either side of his mouth as they shake hands.

They chat for a bit, then the tall guy points at the roof in the direction of my bedroom. I shrink back from the window. But not before I notice the back door of the four-wheel drive open.

A boy steps out. Striped shirt. Ears built for listening.

A flurry of panic scrambles up my throat.

'Hope you don't mind I brought my boy. Good ladder spotter, he is. Eamon, say g'day.'

Eamon wipes his hand on his pants before offering it to Dad. Dad is shaking the boy's hand. The boy he bet me only an hour ago that I'd never see again.

I drop down to the floor between my bed and the window, where nobody can see me.

This is a disaster. They should advertise this stuff on the website. When they say 'isolated cabin', it's not actually isolated.

You will have people creep up on you by the creek and climb on your bedroom roof.

Dad chats away casually as they stop outside my window. Like he's forgotten I was hiccupping from tears not long ago. Like he forgot how he talked me into staying and helped me unpack my suitcase again, with false promises of never having to see another living soul out here.

'That was quite a storm last night.'

The tall man laughs. 'Just a little tickle. They get a bit stronger than that. Come out of nowhere. You get used to it.'

He rests the ladder against the cabin, across my bedroom window, and the eave creaks with his weight. A shadow falls across my room. The tin groans above me and I imagine the tall man falling right through the roof. Landing on my bed. Staring at me.

I steal a glance up at the window. Eamon's holding the ladder.

I suddenly remember all the bedding hanging over the verandah to dry. It must look like I'm a bed-wetter.

'Eamon,' the man calls from the roof. 'Pass me a wrench, would ya?'

Eamon disappears from sight. There's a squeal of metal, then rummaging.

'This the one?' he calls back.

'That's it.'

The eave creaks and another shadow falls across my room.

I look up to see a pair of grubby sneakers climbing the ladder. But just as I'm about to look away, the ladder with the sneakers tilts sideways. There's a groan, and I watch as the ladder, with Eamon still holding on, falls sideways.

It hits the ground with a loud crack.

I shoot up like an arrow and peer through the curtains.

The boy is lying still on the ground.

Dad rushes over. The voice from the roof calls out.

Dad lifts the ladder off Eamon.

'Scarlett!' he yells. 'Scarlett, get out here!'

I don't think about anything except the boy lying on the ground. I don't even think about my face. I just run. Down the hall, out onto the verandah, leaping down the front steps.

The ladder is lying on the earth alongside Eamon. His eyes are open, blinking up at Dad and me. He tries to sit up, but Dad steadies him with a hand on one shoulder.

'Take it easy, buddy,' Dad says.

The man on the roof is crouched on his knees, looking down. 'You alright, son?'

'How many fingers am I holding up?' Dad asks.

'Three.'

'You hit your head pretty hard,' Dad says. 'Are you in pain?'

'Did I fall off?' Eamon asks.

'You did. Do you remember?'

'Not really.'

'Scarlett, go grab an ice pack from the freezer,' Dad says.

I race inside to the kitchen and rummage through the freezer. By the time I return, Eamon is sitting up, resting back with his hands on the dirt. I give Dad the ice pack and he holds it to Eamon's head.

'Could you put the ladder back so I can get down?' the man

on the roof asks.

'Scarlett, takeover,' Dad says. 'Just sit with him.'

So I hold the ice pack to Eamon's head, until his face turns the colour of beetroot.

'I've got it,' he says, reaching up for the pack. 'You're the river dancer.'

'Well, you remember something,' I say.

Of course he wouldn't remember falling off the ladder, but he would remember my private moment.

We both watch as Dad lifts the heavy ladder and rests it firmly against the eave, holding it steady as the man climbs down.

'So, first time you see me, I'm jumping out of a tree. Second time, I'm falling off a ladder,' Eamon says. 'Pretty special, huh?'

I feel my left cheek burning up.

The tall man dismounts from the ladder. Heads straight for Eamon.

'I'm alright, Opa,' he says. He tries to get to his feet, but winces and falls back down.

'Steady,' says the man. 'Let's have a look at that knee.'

Eamon tentatively lifts the leg of his shorts. His knee is shiny and swollen.

'Why don't we take him inside?' Dad says. 'We'll elevate and get some ice on it.'

So Dad and the man help Eamon limp up the steps of the verandah and into the cabin, where he lies on the sunken lounge alongside the far window, his leg propped up by pillows and the ice pack slung across his knee.

'I'm okay,' Eamon says. 'You guys don't need to fuss.'

'Dad knows what he's doing,' I say. 'Let him fuss.'

And when Eamon looks at me, I realise he thinks I'm talking about my injuries, so I quickly correct myself. 'Dad was a boxer.'

'Cool,' Eamon says, looking over at Dad. 'Like, the paid professional kind?'

'Just trust me on this one, buddy. You rest up now, and you'll be very glad in the morning,' Dad says. 'Your swelling won't be too bad by then. Now I'm gonna help your old man finish on the roof, then you two can get home, okay?'

'No problemo,' Eamon says, watching the men retreat back outside. 'Your dad's still pretty built, hey.'

'Like muscly? I guess.'

'Does he still box?'

'He trains amateurs now. Amateurs and me.'

Oops. Didn't mean to say that last bit.

'You can box?' Eamon raises an impressed eyebrow.

'A little. No big deal.'

'Hell yeah, it is. I want to learn.'

My entire left cheek begins to pound. I don't want this strange boy to learn boxing. Not with my dad. Not with me. I'm not learning to box just so that I look cool or can pull funky party tricks. I'm learning so that I can build back half the strength I used to have in my arms with half the muscle I now have left in them. But it's not my duty to explain how rehab works to a guy who has likely never been injured in his life.

After a while, we hear the scuffs of feet on the tin roof at the far end of the cabin.

'So how long are you staying here for?'

'Couple of weeks,' I say. 'Why are you here, anyway? Are you guys the caretakers?'

'This is our land,' he says. 'But we live a bit further round the mountain.'

'So this is *your* cabin?'

'Yeah. Well, all of ours. There are a few of us, but we rent it out. People like to get away from the cities sometimes, you know? But most only stay a night or two. They miss the best stuff. Only so much you can discover in a few days. Like most people don't stay long enough to find Tilly's Hut. You gotta trek to the top of the mountain, along the old goat track. I don't tell people about it, normally. It's kind of a secret spot.'

I think of my secret spot on the roof back home, where I climb to watch the stars peek out.

'Sounds cool.'

'Yeah. But you gotta climb like a mountain goat to get there,' Eamon laughs. 'Opa calls it an adventure for the wildly daring or the wildly desperate. Which do you reckon you are?'

'What?'

'Are you wildly daring or wildly desperate?' His green-speckled eyes flash a challenge at me. But it's a bit of a rude question to ask really, and it depends on the day, so I shrug.

'Well, I reckon I'm wildly daring. 'Specially after that trick I just pulled on the ladder. I can take you up to Tilly's Hut if you want. Show you the way and all that. Views like Everest up there.'

A trek with a boy. The whole idea was to come here and *escape* people. Full stop. No more humans for me. But Eamon doesn't look at me like the kids back home. He doesn't know what I was, and he doesn't seem to care what I am now.

'You're probably no good at trekking, right? City slicker and all. Probably a bit scared.'

'Oh, I'm not scared.'

I'm made of the same stuff as Dad. And that sure as hell isn't fear.

He laughs. Flicks his hair out of his eyes. 'You're wildly daring too then, are you?'

'Ha. Listen, life tried to kill me once already and failed. I'm not scared of any trek.'

Eamon looks at me a second longer than he should. He wants to know the story. Same as everyone else. Well, he's not getting it.

'That ladder just tried to kill me too,' he says with a grin.

'Hardly.'

'I guess we were both lucky!'

After the accident, the doctors said I *was* lucky. Lucky to be alive. But touching the lumpy scars left on my face and feeling the ache of the muscles in my arms, the weakness that stops me holding anything heavy for too long, I don't feel lucky. Sometimes I wish I had died instead. There in that car, on the side of the dual-lane Mitchell Motorway. Much easier to die a pretty girl than to be left living as an ugly one.

'Being alive isn't always lucky,' I say.

'Isn't it?' He seems genuinely baffled.

'No. And I don't trust in luck anyway.'

'Maybe it's best you don't go to Tilly's Hut then,' he says. 'You probably wouldn't make it all the way up anyway.'

'Why not?'

'Well, it's a tough climb and you're a city girl, for starters.'

'Aren't you the one with the injured knee?'

The thing nobody tells you when you have a serious injury is that it's not just you who changes, it's everyone around you. And one of the first things they change are their expectations. I very rarely get in trouble anymore. My teachers, my family, the kids at school, they all tread carefully. People expect you can't do things anymore, like I can't dance anymore. But I could still dance circles round most of the kids at my school. I just choose not to.

This country boy has no idea who he's messing with. No idea of the pain I've known, or the fights I've fought, or the strength that burns inside me like a tiny fire desperate for fuel.

'I'm in,' I say. 'What time tomorrow?'

He grins. 'Alright. Meet you here. Sun up.'

AFTER

The sun is up when I wake, and an old man in a blue collared shirt is standing over me with Gran.

'Pretty little thing, isn't she?' he says.

I've seen so many doctors and nurses now, I can't remember their names, but this one has lost the hair on top of his head and grown it upside down as a beard instead.

He studies a photo on Gran's phone, then looks back at me.

'We want to get this right, don't we?' He smiles down at me. 'She'll want to apply lipstick one day and the lip line can be a bit tricky. How recent is that photo?'

'Two days before the accident. It's the most recent one I have.'

'Mind if I copy it for the plastics team? We've got one of the top paediatric plastic surgeons for the job. She's lucky in that respect.'

Lucky. It's the first time I've heard that word since I woke up.

'Oh, that's a relief,' Gran says. And there's hope in her voice. They're going to make me good as new. 'So they'll do a good job. How bad will the scars be?'

The doctor looks briefly at me, then nods out of the room to Gran.

She follows him and I hear their footsteps retreat, then stop. Low murmuring voices. Dad sits with me, not speaking, just holding my bandaged hand.

When Gran eventually comes back, she's sobbing quietly.

Dad goes to her and wraps one arm around her shoulders, pulling her in tight and holding her a moment.

Gran grabs at a tissue from the box by my bedside. She rests a hand on my leg, gives it a gentle rub.

'You're still our gorgeous girl,' she says.

'Of course she is,' Dad says.

I can barely see through my swollen eyes and the patchwork of gauzes, dressings and bandages covering my head, chest, stomach and arms. I haven't seen a mirror yet, and I'm not sure I want to. I don't need anyone to tell me that this is different, very different, to the time I broke my arm.

Gran rests a hand gently on my hair, kissing me on the dressing above my forehead. She pulls away to look at me and a tear escapes down her cheek. Through my puffy eyes, I search for assurances in hers.

'We have one tough road ahead of us, sweetie.'

I nod.

'But we're going to get you through this.' She purses her lips, then blows her nose into the tissue clenched in her fist.

Dad clears his throat. 'Lucky she's got the blood of champions.'

I want to give him a thumbs up, but can only raise my bandaged fist.

'That's a fighter's fist,' he says. 'And don't you forget it.'

NINE

Forget it. I should just forget it. I don't want to hang out with other kids, especially not a boy. Why did I even agree?

'Nice to have some lights on at last,' Dad says, as the inky night falls over the cabin. 'I thought for a while there we were gonna have to go all old school with kerosene lamps.'

He slumps down beside me on the sunken lounge and we watch the flames rise and fall in the wood fire heater. Amazing that the same element contained here in this space can rage into an inferno in a different space. Flames reach left, then right, bending forward and back, dancing to their own beat. Like I was, down by the stream. Before Eamon humiliated me. Why did I agree to go with him?

Of course, I know why. I know exactly why.

'Know what I like most about this cabin?' Dad looks up at the tin roof, then around the room. 'The rusticness of it. Is that even a word? Rusticness. Sounds better than 'run down'. Or 'dilapidated'. You're the expert on words, champ. How about rusticness?'

'I don't think that's a word.'

'Well, it should be. Old things, hand-built things, they have a certain rustic beauty about them, don't they? Not perfect, but interesting. Different. It would be a different life out here. Simpler, but harder too.'

I'm not really listening. I agreed to the hike because of that look on Eamon's face. I wanted to wipe it straight off his mouth and out of his eyes. He was the definition of smug, and I should know, I've copped enough smug looks from girls like Pippi since I started back at school. Looks that say 'I'm better than you now'.

'Nothing's been done perfectly here, has it?' Dad pulls an orange from the fruit bowl sitting on the coffee table. 'Watch this.'

He holds it to the floor and gently releases his fingers. The orange hesitates a moment before slowly rolling away from Dad, down towards me, then past me, gathering momentum on its way to the bay window.

'I think the whole thing was built crooked,' Dad says, and shrugs. 'But I'm not complaining. It's warm.' He reaches his hands towards the fire. 'And my favourite girl in the whole world is here with me. What's not to like?'

I smile.

'Everything alright, champ?'

I feel funny telling him about my plans with Eamon tomorrow. He might make a crack about me spending time with a boy. He might not even let me.

'It was good you came out and helped with that kid. He could have been hurt real bad. It was brave of you.'

'Brave?'

Am I that awful to look at that coming out in public is an act of bravery?

'I just mean that I know you didn't want to see them. But when he fell, you came out anyway.'

'Mmm, thanks.'

'Something on your mind, champ?'

Ugh, I hate it when parents have that instinct. Surely my own thoughts are allowed to be private? But I guess I do need to tell Dad at some point.

'You know that boy, Eamon?'

'He's the one you saw down by the river, I'm guessing?'

'Yeah. And he's kinda asked me to go hiking tomorrow, up to this place called Tilly's Hut. He basically said he didn't think I could do it, that I probably wasn't strong enough because I'm a city girl.'

'He said that?' Dad raises one eyebrow.

'People don't think I can do stuff anymore, do they?'

'Well, you'll show them you can.'

'Do I look weak to people, do you think?'

'Hell no. Not with those battle scars, you don't. So what did you tell the little twerp?'

'I said yes. I'd do it.'

Dad looks at me a moment. Just when I think he's about to say no way in hell am I going off the beaten track with that boy, he says, 'I hope you told him you'd not only do it, you'd smash it?'

I narrow my eyes. I don't even know if I *can* do it, let alone 'smash it'.

'You'll show him,' Dad says.

'I'll show him alright,' I say quietly.

And just like that, I'm committed.

Not because I told Eamon I would go, or even because I told Dad. I'm committed because I told myself.

A hollow tapping wakes me. Something is wrong.

A spear of light on my pillow.

The sun. It's up!

Another hollow tapping noise down the hall. The singsong of a butcher bird. My heart thuds as I shoot up straight in bed.

I am in my own bed. Not Dad's.

There was no screaming in the night. No nightmares I can remember at all.

The tapping noise starts up again.

My clothes are neatly folded on the floor beside me. Denim shorts, boots and my long-sleeved Ever Dance t-shirt.

I rip off my pyjamas and try not to look at the latticework of scars that start at my stomach and run all the way up my body. But they are impossible to ignore. It's the wrinkly, shiny, patchy skin of an old lady. It doesn't belong to a fourteen-year-old girl, but it's part of me forever now. I pull on my shirt and feel instantly better. Covered. Sun safe is how I need to roll these days.

No time for breakfast, or to fix my hair. I run my fingers through it and tie it back in a rough ponytail. Stuff my drink bottle into my backpack and jam a hat down low over my face.

I catch a glimpse of myself in the bathroom mirror as I leave my room. My ponytail spills over my left shoulder, almost white against my hot pink shirt. At a quick glance, with a hat shielding my face in the dim morning light, I look almost like a regular teenage girl. I make my way down the hall and scrawl Dad a quick note on the kitchen bench.

Gone to prove myself.
– S xx

I pause at the front door of the cabin. Deep breaths, Scarlett, he's already seen your face. My heart still beats a little harder as I ease the door open.

I step onto the verandah, only to be slammed against the cabin wall by my shoulders. Pinned by the paws of a mountain lion or some kind of giant beast. He stands to his full height so that he's taller than me, and licks his long tongue up the side of my face, right over my scars, knocking my hat onto the wooden deck.

'Chief, down!' Eamon says. 'Down, Chief!'

But the dog keeps licking me, from my chin right up to my hairline, his tail wagging furiously, hot doggy breath in my ear.

'Down, boy!' Eamon wrenches him back by the collar to pull him off me. 'Sorry. Are you okay?'

'Yeah,' I laugh, rubbing at my shoulders where I can still feel the pinch of his claws. That dog has no idea how much physio it took to get the movement back in my shoulders. And by the look of it, his care factor is about zero. I pick my hat up off the verandah and quicky jam it back on.

'Well, he obviously likes you,' Eamon says.

I give Chief a pat on his wide head. Golden and shiny with droopy bloodshot eyes and a black muzzle, his shoulders stand taller than my waist.

'What kind of dog is he?' I say. 'Besides a giant, I mean.'

'A bitsa.'

'I haven't heard of that breed.'

Eamon laughs. 'No, it means he's bitsa this and bitsa that. Bit of Great Dane, bit of Bull Mastiff, not sure what else. I thought we could use a tour guide.' He pats his flank. 'He's good at playing mountain goat, aren't ya, boy?'

Chief wags his tail and looks up at Eamon, his salmon tongue hanging out one side of his mouth.

'I was starting to think you'd chickened out of coming,' Eamon says.

'Me?'

'Yeah, I was knocking for ages. Thought you must have changed your mind.'

'No, I'm a bit tougher than that. How about you, though? How's the knee?'

Eamon lifts the leg of his grey shorts. His knee is red, but no longer swollen.

'I think your old man was right about the ice trick.'

'Dad's good with that stuff.' Then I realise again that he probably thinks I'm talking about me. 'Anyway, where's your stuff?'

Eamon's wearing a loose t-shirt with a stretched neck and a few nicks around the shoulders. But he carries no bag, not even a water bottle.

'What stuff?'

'The essentials for life. You know, food, water.'

He laughs. 'Last I checked, water was running in the creek.'

'And what about food? Gum leaves?'

He smiles. 'You always give this much attitude? Or do you just really like me?' He gives Chief a rub across the collar. 'I think she likes me, boy.'

My left cheek betrays me by flushing hot.

'I actually don't like people, as a general rule.' Eamon's face falls briefly. 'Sorry, I didn't mean—'

'No, I'm sorry you lucked out and stumbled across me. But you could do worse, trust me. You don't survive long out here without people. You go a little bit wild. Being alone is overrated.'

'I'd love it.'

But when I really think about living out here all alone, through that storm the other night, never seeing Dad or Gran or Danny or Anna, I know he's right. I would lose my mind.

I follow Eamon and Chief down the verandah steps and into the clearing.

'We're heading that way,' Eamon says, pointing to the west.

I look behind the cabin where Matilda Mountain rises steeply. The morning air is sharp and the tip of the mountain makes a crisp lavender line against an aquamarine sky.

'Right to the very top.'

It looks jagged and steep and very much mountain goat country, like Eamon said. I hope I'm strong enough for this. Please, don't let me embarrass myself. I swallow my doubt and hitch my bag higher on my shoulders.

'Let's go then.'

We set out for the tree line behind the cabin, Chief leading the way. The ground is damp underfoot from the recent rain and Chief's feet kick up clods of earth as he prances ahead of us.

'I'm guessing he knows the way?'

'Like the back of his snout.'

The morning sun is kind, trickling down between the trees, just enough to warm our shoulders. Chief gallops ahead, towards a stone wall at the end of the tree line.

'He's a thirsty boy,' Eamon says. 'Knows where to find the cleanest water in the country.'

Eamon runs after him, a slight limp in the leg he injured yesterday, and I follow.

A soft gurgling can be heard as water trickles down the glossy stone wall from high up on Matilda Mountain somewhere, making a small clear pool on the rocks below, before sliding on downhill.

Chief laps at the pool and Eamon crouches upstream from him, cupping his hands in the water and making slurping sounds as he drinks.

'Who needs to lug a drink bottle around when you have this?' he says.

I pull mine from my pack. Take a long, deliberate sip of it.

'City slicker,' he calls.

'At least I'm not sharing dog germs.'

'Hey, Chief,' Eamon calls, and the great dog lifts his head, jowls dripping with water, ears cocked in question. 'You don't have germs, do you, boy?'

Chief prances over to Eamon and jumps on him. They rumble

on the golden grass until Chief is standing over Eamon, his hand-sized paws either side of Eamon's ears, slobber dripping onto his face.

'Ugh!' Eamon wipes the back of his hand across his face, and I laugh.

'That'll teach you. You're both goofs.'

And I feel light. Normal almost, for the first time since the accident.

Beneath the shade of the tall she-oaks, I am sheltered. Eamon jumps up and dusts the dry grass from his shorts, giving Chief a pat on the rump that sends him running to the right of us and disappearing up a track. The trail is steep and travels between rock shelves, the odd gum tree sprouting crooked between the cracks.

I climb and pant, and Eamon chats about his Aunt Becky, who never stops talking, even to their goats, and his little sister, Cat, who doesn't say much but follows him like a shadow. He talks about Opa, who isn't his real grandad, but who he calls Opa anyway.

'Because being a grandfather is something you do,' Eamon says. 'Not something you just are.'

'You think "grandfather" is a verb?' I say, grabbing hold of a tree trunk to reef myself up onto a stone shelf. I stop to catch my breath, allowing the burning in my biceps to mellow.

A year ago, nobody would have believed I could climb a mountain, or pull myself up onto a ledge the way I just did. A year ago, my arms were thin as twigs, most of my muscle eaten by flames.

'Don't know too much about verbs.'

I think of Dad coaching me through every step of my recovery. Even when he was scared. And bone-achingly tired. And there must have been times he felt like I was a lost cause. But he never showed it.

'You're right,' I say. 'Being a parent or grandparent is something you do. Being a friend probably is too.'

I think of Pippi, who calls herself my friend, and Anna, who really is, even though her honesty hurts.

'Wouldn't know,' Eamon says. 'I don't have many friends, really. Just family.'

'Don't you have friends at school?'

He laughs. 'School? My school is here.'

'Where?'

'On Matilda Mountain. We're homeschooled.'

'Wow. So you don't have to deal with, like, teachers or kids or anything?'

A new idea is forming. Homeschooling on the mountain. Making this stay permanent. I already have half my family here. And Dad did say he thought it would be a simpler life out here.

'Well, there *are* other kids here I have to deal with. Cousins, mostly. But yeah, I like homeschooling. You do get lonely sometimes, though. Seeing the same kids every day. Mostly it's just old couples who come to stay in the cabin, or young couples all kissy and slobbery over each other. Not many families stay, but it's cool when they do. New kids are cool.'

'No, new kids can be cruel.'

We walk on, leaves crunching underfoot, Eamon eerily quiet.

'Do you mind if I ask what it was?'

'What *what* was?' I pretend to be ignorant.

'The thing that tried to kill you?' he says. 'Not that you have to tell me, it's none of my business really. I hope you don't think I'm rude for asking.'

And because of that, because he doesn't expect or think he has the right to know, I find the words.

'I got burnt,' I say.

'I bet it hurt like hell.'

I shrug.

I tell myself I don't remember the flames licking my skin. I tell myself over and over, but I lie.

'Was it a house fire?' he asks softly.

This is what most people assume. Me trapped on the second storey of my house, rescued by some big firefighter, who threw me over his shoulder and carried me down a ladder.

'No. A car.'

My mind flashes back to the accident. To the *before*. If only we'd not been rushing . . . if only I'd not been so stressed about getting to my ballet exam on time . . . if only we'd left the house five minutes earlier or five minutes later . . . if only we'd been in a different lane of traffic . . . if only Gran hadn't locked up the brakes so suddenly. It was a mere matter of seconds. Seconds between that truck slamming into us or not. Seconds between perfect and burnt. Between pretty and ugly.

It's the same old thing, the If Only game. I constantly replay every moment, as if I can somehow tweak one factor and change what happened. Avoid the tragedy. Spare myself the pain, the surgeries, the scars, the damage. Spare Gran and Dad the grief.

But no matter how many times I rearrange it in my head, the *after* happened. Nothing can undo that simple fact: it happened.

'It was a car accident,' I say. 'A semitrailer hit us from behind.'

I shiver, goosebumps dusting my skin.

'It put a hole in the fuel tank, and there must have been a spark. It only takes one spark.'

'Geez.'

'And I was trapped. In the passenger seat.'

I wrap my arms around myself because I'm suddenly cold, cold all over, and my body is trembling.

I have never told this story before. My story. The one I don't want.

Why can I tell a boy I barely know when I could never even tell Anna? Maybe because he doesn't know what I was before, so he doesn't care what I am now. Maybe because I will never have to see him again after we leave. There is a certain freedom in confiding in a stranger. I don't know why it tumbles out. All I know are words. Lots and lots and lots of words. Spilling out of me like they've spent five hundred days plugged up inside. Which I guess they have.

I tell Eamon everything. How the heat in the car was like the inside of an inferno. The kind of heat you can't describe, but only feel. How it sucked all the oxygen from my lungs. How it was hot enough to melt my clothes into my skin, and my skin into my seatbelt. By the time emergency services pulled me out, the skin on my arms slid off like the skin on two overcooked frankfurts.

He listens quietly, doesn't say a word. And I speak more than

I have spoken in seventeen months. The words keep coming as we walk, steeper now, and I'm shaking and panting as we trek up between trees tall as giants. My mouth is dry, but I don't stop for water. We keep walking, and I keep talking.

I tell him how after the doctors saved my life, my body shut down from infection. How I spent twelve days on life support, just breathing in a black world.

I tell him about the day physio started. That was the first day I knew I would live. They wouldn't bother with physio otherwise. It was also the first day I was no longer sure I wanted to live.

I tell him how my arms were somehow thinner in muscle, but thicker in skin. How it took days for me to learn to swallow again and weeks for me to talk again, because the fire had breathed down my throat.

And I tell him how after all of that, when I finally got home from hospital, I had to wear a compression suit to help reduce my scarring. Twenty-three hours of every day, for three hundred and sixty-five days, I wore it. Yeah, well, look at me now. As if those three hundred and sixty-five days of torture made any difference.

'It's been off nearly two months now,' I say.

'So that's why you can dance again,' he says.

'No,' I say. 'I don't dance anymore.'

'Umm . . . I kinda saw you doing something that looked very much like dancing.'

'I'm talking about ballet. On stage. I'll never dance like that again.'

'Why not?'

'Why do you think?'

'I dunno. You looked good the other day. Like a forest fairy.'

I shake my head. 'You don't understand.'

Chief leads the way, snout to the earth, up a dark narrow track which winds through steep bushland and ledges. I cling to these ledges as I carefully plant my feet.

Eamon is ahead of me, deftly putting one foot before the other. I avoid tripping over the roots sticking out of the ground, but my shoulders ache from the weight of my pack.

'Dancing isn't just about being good.' My breathing is laboured now. 'My teacher always said dancing is about three things: grace, expression . . . and beauty. It's also about strength.'

'And you don't have that?'

'Not anymore.'

He says nothing. He's wise to say nothing.

I pull myself up over a flat ledge after Eamon, to where the bush opens into a small clearing. The air is thinner here, grass bleached yellow under a pool of sunshine.

'But it's just your skin.'

I stop momentarily.

'What?'

'It's just the covering.'

I laugh once. Shocked. Bitter. 'Oh no, it's not.'

No, Eamon, what happened to me isn't just about the three layers of my skin. It's about not having full muscle tone in my arms and no longer being able to rely on their strength to rise on the dance floor or pull me up a mountain. It's about not being able to move without contracture scars tightening my skin and muscles and nerves, restricting my movements. It's about pain.

The kind of pain nobody is meant to survive. Pain that makes you scream and shake and cry. It's about losing my face. People are identified by the faces they wear. It's how we recognise each other. And I lost mine. Swapped it for a different face. One that draws stares and comments for completely different reasons. One that has destroyed my regular life as a teenage girl. The girl I was. The girl I really am inside.

The one who used to paint rainbows and butterflies. The one who was told her paintings were beautiful, her hair was gorgeous, her face was pretty. Nobody said Danny's paintings were beautiful. They said, 'What a fine technique, Danny!' 'How clever you are, Danny!' 'How smart you look dressed up in that button-up shirt.'

Everything I did was beautiful in the *before*. A beautiful girl with a beautiful face and a beautiful body doing beautiful paintings and beautiful dances.

But she's gone.

There's no way to compress all the feelings of five hundred days into a parcel I can hand to Eamon. All my words are used up.

And I believed he was different. Silly really. Just because he comes from a pathetic mountain and gets homeschooled, I thought he might understand. Of course he can't. He's just like everyone else who hasn't lived through it.

I can't believe he'd say that after I just told him *everything*.

Nobody, nobody has spoken to me like this since the accident. Everyone at school is so very careful. People move around me and speak to me like I'm made from hand-blown glass.

Nobody has said this is no big deal. Because it is. It is a very big damn deal.

How careless Eamon is. He, who is a boy, and an unscarred one. He can afford to speak in greys. It's not a boy's duty to be beautiful. Whereas I am a girl, and therefore everything I do must bring beauty to the world. People like pretty things, hasn't he heard? And I am no longer one of them. I'm nothing more than a smudge. A smudge in a perfect world.

'Scarlett, come on,' Eamon calls from somewhere up ahead.

I pick up my feet and they surge forward with new energy. Angry energy. How dare this boy who is whole tell me that my burns are just about my skin!

But when I follow the track around a bend, I forget about my skin. Don't have any thoughts about skin at all. Because I am standing before a hut on the edge of the world.

The girl who almost lost her right arm to an infection just climbed a mountain.

AFTER

Each day I climb a mountain. This is how it feels.

Each morning I learn what real pain means.

Each morning, when the nurses arrive.

Here they come now. I can hear their footsteps down the hall.

Pitter-patter. Soft, gentle.

Prickles of fear down my spine. My body trembles.

I am crying already. Crying because I know what's about to happen to me.

The door is eased closed. Two nurses pad forward.

'Where would you like us to start?' they ask.

There is no good place to start. There is no part of me which hurts less when my dressings are ripped off and reapplied.

Every single time, it is like they are peeling off my skin and rubbing sandpaper into my raw, oozing wounds. Every single time I scream.

'My face,' I say. 'Start with my face.'

Because my face is the worst. The most hated. Start with that.

'Ready?'

I nod.

I am never ready. Nobody could be ready to be skinned alive.
One nurse holds me. The other peels back my dressing.
A high-pitched animal noise.
I *make these noises. Screams from a burning hell.*
'I'm sorry,' the nurse says. 'Ready again?'
My armpit is sweaty. Sweaty with fear.
I grit my teeth and nod.
She peels off my skin.
Pain lives inside me and outside me and all around me.

TEN

Around me, the wind falls still. Hushed for a moment, like I am, looking at the view.

Short and squat, the hut has a peaked wooden roof that sweeps down either side to almost touch the ground. Facing us is a wonky log staircase leading up to a solid timber door.

Beyond the hut, far off in the distance, the hills sleep in a haze against an indigo sky.

'Tilly's Hut, at your service,' Eamon says.

Chief sniffs the dry grass sticking up in clumps at the corner of the log staircase. He cocks his leg and looks out over the valley as he wees on it.

'Try teaching him the meaning of sacred,' Eamon says, climbing the staircase up to the door of the hut. 'You coming?'

Eamon is at the top step as I climb the first, feeling the wood groan under my weight. Then he is heaving open the door, which seems to drag along the floor.

I follow him inside the cool darkness. It smells of damp wood and dust, and spider webs are laced across its roof, but otherwise it's neat and tidy. A flat timber desk perches beneath a window that has views back towards the coast. From here, the ocean is a strip of glitter. A small ocean, beneath a heroic cobalt sky.

Tucked beneath the table is a chair. Wooden, short, simple—made, not bought.

'How old is this place?' I whisper. Because ancient and solitary things require reverence.

'Old—like a hundred years or so.'

'Whose was it?'

'Tilly's, of course,' he says. 'That's a no-brainer.'

I feel myself blush. 'Oh, well, yeah. But I mean, who was she?'

'Besides being the person who first started our village, she was a writer. Or so Mum says anyway.'

I run my hand gently across the top of Tilly's grainy desk, and it comes back to me black.

'She had a great view. I wonder what she wrote about.'

'I'd have to ask Mum again. She did tell me once.'

The hut is small enough for Eamon and I to walk a few paces from one end to the other. It has windows on two sides, wide open to the wind and the rain, but protected by the low-sweeping wooden roof.

There's a scuffle, then a skid, as Chief mounts the stairs and leaps in after us. His breath is hot and his panting loud as his tail whips my legs.

He looks up at Eamon, tongue lolling out one side of his mouth.

'You're not meant to come in here and you know it,' Eamon says.

Chief whines, as if to say, *But I go everywhere with you*,

and Eamon softens. Tousles his big head.

'Alright, I'm getting ravenous,' he says. 'Want to have lunch at mine?'

I bend down and scratch Chief's ears to avoid the question. There is a part of me that's curious to see where he lives, and how he survives on this mountain. I get the feeling his family is different, and not just because of the homeschooling. I feel like they might just be living my dream: isolated mountain life. And if they are, I need to learn all about how they do that so I can explain it to Gran and Dad. It's obviously possible.

'My people are pretty cool, if that's what you're worried about. They're not scary. My sister wouldn't even notice you.'

'Really?'

'Really. She doesn't say much.'

I take a deep breath. 'Okay, then.'

'You'll come?'

I nod. This is a research trip. Hopefully I can deal with the staring and the soft pitying eyes if it means I'm a step closer to making this kind of isolation my forever.

Eamon doesn't have a house. That's the first thing I notice as we come over the hill and down to his . . . camp? Village? Caravan park?

A cluster of brightly coloured caravans and shipping containers with verandahs welded on are scattered in a rough circle in a clearing at the bottom of the rise.

'Ours is the one with the flowers.'

My mouth is dry suddenly, and my heart is beating me a warning. This is not what I had in mind. 'How many people live here?'

'Just me and my family,' he says. 'There are twenty-three of us.'

'That's a lot of people.'

'It's alright, you won't meet them all. The kids are in school—that's the bright blue building you can see over there.' He points to one of the shipping containers. 'Everyone else is working till lunch. Except Mum and Cat.'

'Where does everyone work?'

'Here.' He says it in an obvious way, like where else would they work?

'What does everyone do?'

He laughs. 'It's a lot of work to live self-sufficiently, so we have a roster system. But mostly we work outside with the crops. Or Opa drives to town to sell fruit and veggies at the markets. Oh, and I'm the family fisherman,' he says, his narrow chest rising slightly. 'I've gotten so good I can feed everyone at least once a week.'

I think back to his spot in the willow tree. 'I thought you were fishing for fun.'

'That too.' He grins. 'But it's my job.'

We're almost at the camp now, and a faint moaning sound grows louder as we approach.

'Damn,' he says under his breath.

'What?'

'Cat. My sister.'

'What about her?'

'Sorry in advance. She might be in a bit of a prickly mood. She does this. Just don't take any offence. Come on.'

He takes off running, Chief streaking ahead of him. I falter behind. The moaning isn't exactly the most welcoming sound. The camp site is deserted, except for a cluster of chickens that flap away as we approach. The moaning rises and falls.

Eamon waits for me at the steps of the caravan with the bright pink and orange flowers all over it. The paint is peeling, and the colours look more faded than they did from a distance. He pulls back the door and walks up the narrow steps into the caravan, then beckons to me.

'Mum, I brought a friend. Hope you don't mind.'

The moaning rises drastically. Turns to shrieking. A terrifying, wild animal sort of noise.

'What friend?' A woman's voice, clear and smooth and quiet.

I follow Eamon inside the caravan, which has a small table to one side with a tight, L-shaped lounge around it and a couple of bunk beds off to one end of the van. A woman with long braided hair stands beside the beds, stroking someone.

Lying on the top bunk is a girl. The girl's face is wet as Eamon rushes over to her. She looks briefly at him, then away again. Her face is exquisite. Chocolate eyes framed with thick full lashes, and an even thicker braid twisting, crown-like, across the top of her head. Full lips and a dainty red nose. I feel an instant pang of jealousy.

'Has she been going all morning?' he asks.

'Aren't you going to introduce me to your friend?' his mum says.

'Oh, yeah, sorry. Scarlett, this is my mum, Claudia.'

'Hi,' I say.

'Welcome, Scarlett.' His mum smiles at me until I dip my head to break eye contact.

'And this naughty little lady here,' Eamon taps on the edge of the bed, 'is my sister, Cat. I think someone was jealous that I went off without her.'

The moaning begins again, and I watch Cat writhe on the bed a moment, biting down on the palm of her hand.

'Hey, I'm back now, enough of that.' She quiets at his voice. 'Sorry, Mum, I should have taken her.'

Eamon soothes Cat with his hand on her hair, until she is quiet. I wonder if she's sleeping.

'I'll make you kids tea,' Claudia says, leaving Cat to Eamon. She swishes past me in her long button-up dress and sets about filling the kettle and turning it on. 'Take a seat, sweetie. You eat zucchini slice?'

'Sure.'

I slide into the seat behind the table.

While the kettle boils, Claudia sidles back past me to the bunk beds. 'Feeling better, possum? I'll make you a nice cup of tea, hey?'

'Come on, up you get,' Eamon says.

A long thin figure slinks down out of the top bunk. She's almost as tall as Eamon, but not quite. Eamon slips onto the lounge seat beside me, and Cat squashes in next to him.

Cat looks past Eamon at me, her dark eyes flitting across mine.

'Hi,' I say.

She looks away again.

'Like I said, she doesn't talk much,' Eamon says.

'But she is the world's best secret keeper,' his mum says, pouring four mugs of tea into tin cups. 'Cat knows everyone's secrets, don't you, Cat?'

Cat hums a tune to herself, picking at the metal edging on the table as Claudia slides the mugs towards us all, along with plates of thick zucchini slice. She hasn't looked twice at my face. Neither of them have.

'So tell me,' Claudia says, cupping her tin in both hands, 'how are you finding it on our mountain?'

'She loves it,' Eamon says.

'Let her talk!'

'I love it,' I say, and the three of us laugh. 'No, really, I could seriously live here.'

'Except she doesn't like people,' Eamon says. He raises his eyebrows at me. 'As a general rule.'

I feel my cheek start to throb. That sounds really bad. Ungrateful.

'It's not like that.' I sip my tea and almost scald my tongue.

Claudia shrugs. 'Cat doesn't much like people either, does she, Eam?'

'Nope.'

'Is the cabin comfortable enough? Got enough wood to stay warm?'

'It's perfect. Exactly what I needed.'

Claudia will take in my scars now, start piecing together my story in her own way.

'I bet it's good to escape,' she says wistfully. 'I think we could all do with a bit of an escape from real life sometimes.'

Surely she's already escaped from real life out here? You can't get much further away than the middle of nowhere.

'I've been very lucky really,' Claudia says. 'Two gorgeous kids with not a mean bone in either of their bodies. Sure, Cat can be a bit difficult sometimes, can't she, Eam?' Eamon nods and sips his tea. 'But we sure do love her. Any of us would die for her, wouldn't we, Eamon?'

'We sure would.'

A chill creeps down my spine. They speak so flippantly of dying. They don't know the panic of those final moments.

'So Eamon told me he was taking you up to Tilly's Hut. Gorgeous little spot, isn't it? Did he tell you about Tilly?'

'Course I did,' Eamon says. 'But I can't remember the book.'

'Tilly was an interesting character,' Claudia says. 'I often wish I could sit down over a cup of tea with her and ask her a few questions. A woman living alone on a mountain in the 1920s was an unusual thing.' She sips her tea and lowers her voice. 'It was grief that brought her here. Her husband died in the First World War, and Tilly and her daughter caught the Spanish flu not long afterwards. Only Tilly survived. Legend has it that after she buried her daughter, Tilly couldn't stand to live in their family home anymore, which was full of her daughter's handprints and dolls and shoes. So she left the city for the mountains. Well, for *this* mountain. Which became *her* mountain, where she lived the rest of her days.'

Claudia makes it sound so easy. To just pack up your old life and move. Maybe it *is* that easy. Why do Dad and Gran have to make out it's such a big deal?

'Nobody knows how she built her hut. Who carried the materials, and how. It's all a bit of a mystery.' She shrugs and smiles sadly. 'But what we do know is that Tilly would go up to her hut every day, religiously, and spend a few hours sitting at that desk in there, writing. In her diary, she said it was her writing that saved her. She couldn't have survived without it. So she bled the pain in her heart out onto the blank pages, and those pages eventually made a book that found its way to a little publishing house in the backwaters of Sydney. But Tilly died before the book was published. She never lived to see it or hold it in her hands.'

'What was the book called?' I ask.

'It was called *Wings*. I read it to you, Eamon, but maybe you were too small to remember?'

Eamon shrugs. 'I don't remember.'

'It's a story about a girl who is gravely ill and wants to fly far, far away from her mountain home. So every day she hikes to the top of the mountain and listens to the birds, calling to them, pleading with them. "Please give me wings so that I may fly far, far away, like you," she says. The little girl's parents don't know she hikes up the mountain, but she does it every single day. Like a pilgrimage. Even when it's raining and the path is slippery with mud. Because she'd heard that if you wish for something hard enough and often enough, if you *really* sweat for it, your wish goes out into the universe. And the power of that wish joins with the universe, and sometimes, just sometimes, if that power is strong enough, your wish may come true.'

I have stopped sipping my tea, entranced by Claudia's voice.

'Well, it started small. The girl began growing fine downy hairs all over her body, and the hairs grew until they became feather-like. All the while, the little girl's body grew thinner. But she kept climbing the mountain. Even though she ate less each day, even though she became frail and thin, even though her bones hollowed out like a bird's, she climbed. Until one day, the girl could barely walk. Still, she dragged herself painstakingly up the mountain. And this time, when she reached the top, she did what she had been working up the courage to do for a long time.

At the top of the mountain, along the crown of a sheer rocky cliff, there grew a gum tree. Tall and strong and smooth was its trunk. Low were its branches. So she clawed her way onto the lowest branch. It took hours, but she clung and she climbed, foot by foot and limb by limb, up to the top bough of the tree. Up to where the lorikeets screeched and the galahs snuggled. Of course, the birds scattered long before she had reached that top bough—the bough that stretched over the steep drop off the mountain and into the valley.

There the girl made her wish once more. "Let me fly far, far away, like the birds." The girl did not look down into the valley below. She put her faith in the universe, stretched out her arms, and leapt.'

'And what?' Eamon says.

Claudia shrugs. 'That's where the story ends.'

'Pfft. That's not an ending! Did she fly or did she die?'

'What do you think?'

'You're the one who read the story!'

'You think everything has a scripted ending?' Claudia laughs.

'Oh, Eamon, surely life in this family has taught you that there are many ways a story can end. None of us really control how our story starts, but sometimes we get to decide how it ends. Maybe Tilly was leaving the ending open. Maybe she was letting us decide for ourselves. How would you end the story?'

'Not with the girl dying,' I say.

The words are out before I realise and I'm suddenly embarrassed by my desire for this small bird-girl to live. I clutch my mug a little tighter in my hands.

'No, she would fly,' Eamon says with certainty. 'Nobody would end the story with a little girl falling to her death.'

'I hope she did fly,' Claudia says. 'There are other possibilities, of course.'

'Yeah?'

'Maybe the story wasn't finished before it was published. Maybe Tilly hid the final pages somewhere. Some people say the final pages were lost, or that Tilly herself was lost. But I believe she did it on purpose. I like to think it was an act of hope.' Claudia smiles and her eyes sparkle. 'Have you ever wanted something so badly . . .' She stops, and a quiver crosses her face. There are tears in her eyes as she looks at Cat, who hums to herself, still picking at the metal edge of the table.

'Sometimes I wish she wasn't this way,' Eamon says under his breath.

'But then she wouldn't be her, would she?' Claudia says.

'I do love her,' Eamon says. 'I love her more than anyone.'

Claudia reaches for his hand across the table.

'She knows, Eam, she knows.'

Cat tips back the last of her tea, and pushes her mug away. Claudia gathers up our plates and cups, all empty now, and runs water into the miniature sink.

'I'll do that,' Eamon says, getting up.

Claudia kisses him on the cheek, gives me a little smile. 'He's about as good as they come.'

'Mum, stop.' Eamon turns away to the sink, the back of his neck crimson.

I know what that feels like.

'Thanks for the lunch,' I say, to divert attention from Eamon.

'Any time. And as for you, missy,' she says to Cat, 'you and I need to collect the eggs.'

I grab a tea towel hanging above the sink and start drying the dishes. Everything inside the caravan feels shrunken. I can't imagine living in a space so cramped and being as happy as Eamon seems to be.

'How does the van go in a storm?' It sounds rude the second I've uttered it. 'I only ask because it felt like the roof was going to tear straight off the cabin the other night, and the cabin's solid timber. So I just wondered, out here . . .'

'Yeah, the cabin was built right in the path of the trade winds. Great views, but, like Tilly's Hut, it cops the brunt of the wind. It's why we couldn't live there. Plus there were too many of us. So we set up here instead. Protected by the valley. Lower down, so it can flood sometimes, but at least we don't get torn apart.'

As I'm drying the last mug, Claudia returns with Cat, each holding a handful of eggs. I rest the mug in the drying rack. I feel like I'm taking up space in their already crowded little house.

'Well, I should probably head back,' I say, wiping my hands dry on my shorts.

'Let me pack these up for you first.' Claudia places the eggs into a carton. 'And tell your dad I said thanks for helping Eamon yesterday.' She turns to Eamon. 'Why don't you ask Scarlett and her dad over tomorrow night for the gathering?'

Chief trots ahead with Cat, never leaving her side. Eamon couldn't leave her behind twice in the one day.

'So what exactly is "the gathering"?' I ask, as we walk up the hill to the cabin.

'Just a night where all the family get together to eat and play games and talk. You'd have fun . . . even if you don't like people as a rule.'

I roll my eyes. 'Well, I like *your* people. Your people are nice. They don't . . .'

'Make a big deal?'

'Yeah.'

'My people are happy. Happy people don't need to make a big deal.'

We walk on in silence for a while, the afternoon sun splashing our faces.

'So do you want to come?'

Chief has stopped at the cabin and is watching Cat, who is prancing, happy as a deer.

'I'll think about it.'

I say goodbye and watch from the shade of the verandah as Eamon, Chief and Cat disappear into the golden sunshine around the bend.

Then I head inside, call out 'Hi' to Dad and make for my room. Grab my paints, my paper.

I get to work.

Furiously, I blend in the landscape, the mountain, Tilly's Hut. I need to remember what the top of the world looked like. When I'm finished, I stand back and study my painting.

Something is missing.

I go back to my palette. Dab in shades of brown for branches, a few splashes of green for leaves. I take the finest brush in my collection. Ink it with black paint. Then small stroke by small stroke, I paint her in. Long and slender and fairy-like. Balancing on the furthest branch at the top of the world. A silhouette, with feathers on her back and arms outstretched.

AFTER

My right arm is outstretched. Bound to a bed.
They shaved off slices of my skin. Stretched it thin.
New skin to grow in place of the old.
But skin grafts take and skin grafts don't.
This one hasn't. The one on my arm.
Rejected skin. Infected skin. Injected skin.
Clear fluid lines running in; yellow fluid lines running out.
It burns. It burns. It burns.
My arm is on fire.
I sleep.
I wake.
Fire lives inside me.
Nurses in, nurses out of the operating theatre.
Cold fingers, hot arm.
Doctors in.
'What's your name, sweetie?'
'Scarlett.'
'Scarlett what?'

'Lee.'

'How old are you, Scarlett?'

'Thirteen,' I whisper.

'Okay, sweetie, I'm the orthopaedic surgeon, and I'm just going to have a look at this arm. We're going to do our best to save it for you, okay?'

I nod. I need my arm. Both arms. Dancers need arms.

'Now I need you to breathe in this gas for me and count backwards from ten.'

A mask covers my mouth, my nose. It smells sickly sweet.

'Ten . . .'

My eyes are heavier than sand.

'Nine . . .'

I am gone.

ELEVEN

I am gone before Dad wakes. Before the sun can shoot its beams across the mountain.

Following yesterday's track. Alone this time. Armed only with a backpack and a ray of trust. I haven't brought a water bottle. The mountain will water me. I have brought something more precious in my backpack. Paints and brushes and thick absorbent paper.

The trek is longer than I remember from yesterday. Cooler, darker in the undergrowth. The sun, when it rises, is blanketed behind cloud and barely warms the earth. But it's okay, because the walking warms me plenty. The gripping onto small tree trunks as I pass warms my hands, my arms, stretching out my muscles. Like the physios did to me. Bit by slow bit, they stretched out my muscles so that my body could learn how to move again. Learn how to hold a fork again, and lift food to my mouth again. Grab hold of a drink bottle again, and raise it to my lips. And when the physios were finished with me, Dad really got started. 'No excuses, champ,' he'd say. And every morning, we'd head out to the yard for a session of jabs, crosses and hooks. First small movements, nothing that could be called a punch. Then raising my arms higher, as my strength slowly built and my range of movement increased.

I reach the stream where Chief and Eamon drank yesterday, and, without them here to tease me, I copy. Sinking to my knees, I bend towards the running water. My reflection catches me off guard, but the water is rippling over pebbles, my face distorted and indistinct. And what I see doesn't look foreign. I cup handfuls of the clear mountain water to my mouth. It is pure and icy on my hands and on my lips, dribbling down my chin. I smile to myself, then push up off the moist earth, brush the dirt from my knees and keep going. Round the bend and up the steep incline. Rocks slip underfoot, but I grit my teeth and hold onto the branches as I climb. The same way I held onto the bars in the rehab centre at the hospital. Gripping and pulling myself forward.

My legs burn, my arms ache, and there is nobody to talk to or distract me or laugh with. But this is what I wanted, right? A mountain to myself.

By the time I'm standing outside Tilly's Hut, I am panting and drained of energy. Maybe two days of hiking was too much. Since the accident, I keep expecting my body to do everything it could do before, in the same easy way. But my body often feels like an old lady's, all stiff and sore and tired.

I climb the three steps to the door of the hut and push it open. A rush of wind greets me and I open my jacket, letting it cool my chest.

The desk sits patiently waiting for me by the window. I stroke the timber again, heavy and solid and grainy. It will make a nice texture against my paper.

I line up my paints and brushes, then sit down to study the scene out the open window. My art teacher always says time staring out a window isn't time wasted for a creative person. It's a time of dreams, thoughts, visions, the neurons firing. She encourages us to sit in silence and stare out at the world. My heart slows to a patter as I take in this new world. The sea, a dull green moss beneath an ashen sky, but as I watch, a shaft of sunshine sneaks through the cloud base, spearing a handful of rays into the ocean and making it sparkle.

I start with the sea, green and flecked with white in a feeble attempt to capture its sparkle. This time, the sky is not my hero, but a dark broody strip across the paper. The rolling hills kiss the edges of the page. Golden light drips into the sea from a darkened sky. Finally, I paint the windowsill around the edges of the paper. *Inside Looking Out*, I will call it.

And in this painting, there is beauty. Not the butterflies and rainbows kind, the moody kind. Beauty can be tormented too. When I'm finished, I sit in Tilly's chair, gazing out the window of her hut, like I am a queen living in my own solitary queendom. Is this how Tilly felt? How many days did she watch the changing sea from this unchanging window? How many people watched it after her? Why didn't she finish the bird-girl's story?

There is a drawer beneath Tilly's desk, and for one brief moment I wonder if Tilly might have left the final pages of her story inside them. I pull at the drawer, but it's stuck. It takes some tugging and patience before it opens a crack. Then, in small stiff movements, I wrench it open enough to reach my hand inside.

There are no loose pages of an unfinished story. Of course there aren't. But there is something else. Something rectangular and thick. I pull it out.

A notebook, the leathery brown cover cracked and bendy, the page edges worn.

I open the front cover. The first page is dated 3 March 1921.

The sky aches. Clouds heavy as bruises stain the heavens. The sea is tossed and restless. Does darkness know no end? Why must it rain on my little girl in her bed beneath the earth? Cruel, cold world. All I want is her. Warm and plump, breaths rising and falling, the echo of her laughter. The sweet smell of her skin. Instead my cries echo off the mountain. And they are primal, inhuman.

Did she know how much I loved her? From the moment I saw her face, frowning brow, eyes open and watchful as she studied her new world, searching my eyes with her own. Did she know my love from the first to the last? Did she know my love even through my cross words and desperate sorrows? Perfect or broken, I wanted her to stay.

They told me yes, they told me no, they told me let it be so. How can it be so that she is gone? I have failed her. It was my duty to protect her from suffering in this world, and I failed.

If I was a painter, I would paint her perfect face. Perfect because it belonged only to her. The one face I will never again find in this world. I can't make her again inside me, build her to life. I have only my words to paint her. And they are imperfect. Nevertheless, I will cloak her in these words, in my story. I will draw her in letters everywhere I go, so that I may find a world where I can exist with her again.

I shut the diary. Can't read anymore. Sadness is leaking from the pages into my soul, and I don't need more sadness. I put the notebook back and wedge the drawer shut. I feel ashamed for having read Tilly's thoughts. Tilly, who is every bit as dead as her little girl now, but whose pain is still alive on those pages.

Gran wanted a pretty little girl. One with ribbons and curls and ballet slippers. But Tilly? She just wanted *her* girl. Tilly was sorry for not protecting her girl, even though it wasn't her fault she died. Has Gran ever felt sorry, even once, for not protecting me?

I pack my paints, palette and brushes back inside their zip-up bag, but leave my painting to dry on the desk. Then I step outside and find the clouds have parted and the sun is blanketing the world in a golden glow.

When I look back at the hut, it's alight from the half-open door to the peak of the roof. A magpie hops along the timber ridgeline, happy and warm. There is no tree to climb at the edge of Matilda Mountain for any little girl who might like to fly. There is only Tilly's Hut.

I lay down my bag and study the roof, which hangs low to the ground on each side of the hut. Before I can think about it, I am reaching to grip the gutter, pulling myself up the timber slats, grunting and working my arms. Until it's like I'm back home, in my own secret place on the top of the world, watching the sky.

The magpie has fled, but wrens flit between the trees on either side of the clearing below in flashes of blue and yellow.

I stand up on the peak, arms outstretched either side of me. Balancing my weight.

Then I close my eyes, let the sunlight pour deep into my skin.

No longer a scarred girl, but a bird. And I walk the ridgeline as if along a balance beam.

I open my eyes and pivot around. A pirouette on high. Then I raise one leg and wobble. But I'm not scared. I steady myself, leg pointing skyward, leg down. Against the morning sun, I imagine myself a silhouette dancing across the rooftop.

That's when the music starts in my head.

Bird Set Free.

I pick up from where I left off by the stream. Point my toes and walk the full length of the ridge, flick my hands out in time with the beat. I am moving without real thought, moving by heart. I stop thinking and let my body dance to the beat inside me. I leap in a tour jeté, and my heart jumps when my feet find the centre beam. I've not tried the tour jeté since the *before*. I can't believe I just tried it on a roof, and landed it! My heart hammers from the rush. My entire body trembles with the thrill of it. I turn and walk the ridgeline again, arms out to balance me, dancing in step to the song in my head. Before me, the rolling hills are an endless stage, above me, the sun burns like a spotlight, behind me, the trees watch on.

I am Scarlett, watch me dance.

But then my foot slips. I stumble.

Feet sliding beneath me, I catch hold of the timber ridgeline with my fingertips. Clawing on, I drag myself back up, arms straining, shaking. I sit on the peak a moment, arms holding on to the slats on either side to steady me, breathing slowly to calm my heart. Like I have done so many times in the third cubicle of the girls' toilet block at school.

But my heart doesn't race because I fell. It races because I danced.

The lights on Dad's ute cut a beam across the shadowy dirt track as we drive to Eamon's place. A mob of kangaroos bound out of our way and Dad slows down.

The sun hangs heavy above the mountain, only moments left of her light, but the sky has been washed clean of the clouds from this morning.

Dad finally shaved after four days of growing his whiskers, and he's wearing a long-sleeved collared shirt that covers up his tatts. Dad always covers his tattoos when he meets new people and only lets them out once he's comfortable. I wish I could do the same with my scars, but a face isn't the sort of thing you can hide until you feel safe. You have to wear it however it comes.

As Dad slows to a stop outside Eamon's camp, my stomach clenches. It is swarming with people. Little people, big people, old people, young people. There's some kind of cricket game going off on a field behind the caravans, two kids fighting a tug of war over something outside one caravan door, men and women ferrying steaming ceramic dishes in and out of open doorways. I count around two dozen people. New people. And there is nothing for me to hide behind.

'This was a mistake,' I say to Dad.

'You'll be fine.'

Dad opens his door, gets out before I have a chance to protest.

He slams it shut. I stay inside the cab, but it's too late. We were spotted the moment we arrived. Foreign guests, in a foreign car.

Opa comes straight over, shakes Dad's hand. He looks in the cab at me, and Dad comes to my side to open the door. I have no choice but to climb out.

'Eamon,' Opa calls, then turns to me and smiles. 'I hear you've been getting acquainted with our mountain.'

I smile awkwardly, unsure how to respond. I'm thankful when Eamon emerges from his caravan and jogs over to us.

'Hey, c'mon, I'll show you round,' he says to me. 'This time I can give you the proper tour.'

Little kids peep out from inside caravans as we pass, and Eamon points out where his Aunt Becky lives and where his old Uncle Paul lives on his own.

'But nobody's ever really alone here,' he says. 'As you can see.'

Kids drop cards and skipping ropes to watch us pass, but then carry on again afterwards, like it's not such a big a deal that Dad and I are here.

'If you need the bathroom, just follow the stones.'

'Stones?'

He reaches down and picks up a flat yellow stone. 'These. They're solar charged, to light the way to the bathroom. We're on a waterless system. All ecologically sustainable. Opa designed it himself.'

Eamon leads me inside the blue shipping container he pointed out the other day, with the verandah welded to the front.

'Welcome to our humble school,' he says.

I pop my head inside. Beanbags are piled in one corner, and a handful of desks and chairs are scattered around. The front of the room is lined with floor-to-ceiling shelves, brimming with books.

'Cool.'

A bell clangs nearby.

'Dinnertime,' Eamon says. 'That's the kids' bell. Come on.'

I follow him out and see a handful of smaller kids heading for another shipping container. Above the cut-out door, someone has painted the words 'Village Hall'.

Two kids duck in front of us as we approach. A boy with a freckled face and tousled blonde hair and a wild-looking little girl with grubby cheeks, piercing blue eyes and two knotted ponytails.

The girl whispers to the boy, their big eyes staring at me. I shrink from their gaze.

'They're not used to strangers,' Eamon says.

But he's just being kind. Kids that age haven't learnt to hide their shock.

Inside the shipping container, along the left side, is a long table with steaming dishes lined up. And opposite the table, about a dozen log stumps are perched in a semicircle for seats.

'Curry night,' Eamon says.

The little kids seem to know what to do, grabbing a plate from the left and moving along the table, serving themselves steamed rice and curry.

'Fish, lentil or vegetable,' Eamon says. 'You should try the fish. The best fisherman in the village caught it.' He grins.

The young girl who pushed in front of us earlier is ahead of me in the line for food, and as I pile up my plate, she turns around and studies me.

''Scuse me,' she says. 'What happened to your face?'

I feel myself blanch. People aren't usually that blunt.

'That's rude, Heidi,' Eamon says gently. 'It's none of your business.'

'It's okay,' I say. I know everyone thinks it anyway. 'I got burnt.'

It's the second time I've said it now, and the words don't grind as much.

'Whoa.' The girl's blue eyes widen. 'That must've really hurt.'

'Yeah,' I say. 'It did.'

Something releases inside me. I said it. Getting burnt hurt. The whole process hurt. It hurt more than anything else I'll ever know.

'You must've been really lucky not to die!' she says in awe. 'Fires can kill, you know.'

'Heidi!' Eamon says.

I don't know what to say to that, but, in the end, I don't need to say anything, because she rushes over to the boy she came in with and relays my story to him, still wide-eyed.

Eamon and I sit down on a couple of the sawn-off log pieces and eat indoors. A few more young kids come and go, casting glances my way, but nobody else approaches me. We empty our plates and wash them using detergent and hot water from a boiler in the corner of the hall.

As we head outside, night is inking the sky. The edges of the mountains are singed orange from the dying day and stars are piercing the heavens with hope.

A couple of kids run past us.

'Marshmallow time!' they yell.

A light breeze ripples and with it comes a tune.

I haven't heard any music since the drive here, and it pulls at my heart. We follow the littler kids to the source of the sound. In the clearing between all the caravans is a circle of long wooden logs. Sitting on the furthest log to my right is Eamon's mum, Claudia, her eyes closed as she strums at a well-worn guitar, her voice soft and clear.

Cat dances to her own rhythm behind Claudia, twirling in circles as her mum plays.

I am awestruck by the power of the music. By the beauty of Claudia's bright patchwork skirt sweeping her bare toes, her hair hanging in a loose braid over one shoulder.

That's when I notice Dad, just behind me. He's stopped talking and is watching Claudia too. He's staring at her like he can see nobody else. Not even me, watching him.

Maybe that's how I miss the first spark of fire beside me.

Why I jump at the whoosh of flames against my back.

Why I cower from the bonfire that reaches into the dark sky, showering sparks down around me.

Cat squeals, Claudia strums carelessly and bare feet dance in the dirt around the blaze. Heat kisses my skin, naked flames.

Above me, a fire dragon reaches. Roaring, crackling.

Flames. Rushing, reaching.

Cat twirls to her own beat.

Closing in. Leaping, dancing, twisting.

Marshmallows on sticks.

Burning rubber.

Hands reaching towards the flames.

Gran reaching.

Screaming, leaping kids.

A woman screaming. Gran. Still reaching.

I'm not scared of fire. Fire is just oxygen and fuel colliding.

'Get her out! She needs air!'

Just light and heat.

No pain. Just heat, thick as soup.

I'm not scared of fire, Pippi. I'm not.

Amber, yellow, crimson, blue.

Just destruction. Fire can destroy everything.

Me fighting inside.

I cower away from the blaze, breathing hard, dragging air into my lungs, my breaths raspy and ragged.

Heat. Smoke. Heavy chest.

Sweat prickles across my body, a trickle down my back, the banging of my heart in my throat.

Fists on glass. Banging.

Don't they know? Don't they know what can happen?

'Get her out, get her out, get her out!'

How their soft skin can be charred and scarred?

Tugging. Hands gripping, pulling.

How that skin can slide right off their perfect little bones?

Skin sliding down my arms.

Far away, an underwater voice warbles, 'Scarlett, are you okay?'

'Stay with me, little girl. Stay with me.'

Waterlogged sounds in slow motion.

Voices. Soft, loud, louder, more frantic.

Fuzzy vision closes in.

'She's fading.'

Dark sky. Orange sky. Dark . . . Orange . . .

Blue sky. Black sky. Blue . . . Black . . .

My vision tunnels, white strobe lights flash.

AFTER

Lights flash on.

'You ready for your workout?'

'No.'

'You'll be weightlifting before you know it.'

'I don't weightlift.'

'What is it you like to do then?'

'Nothing.'

'Do you like to swim?'

'No.'

'What about drawing? You like to draw, surely?'

'No.'

'Are you a runner? These look like muscly legs. You need your arms for running too.'

I shake my head.

'Let me guess. These are dancing legs? You'll be dancing up a storm again in no time.'

I want to punch her. If I could only bend my arm and make a fist.

No, today's lesson is how to hold a spoon. How to purse my lips.

She cheers when the spoon stays in my fingers longer than two seconds.

'What a champion!'

'Don't call me that.' Only Dad calls me that.

Champions climb big mountains. They don't wobble a spoon in their fingers.

'Come on now, positive thoughts, Scarlett.'

'I wish you'd all let me die.'

'We won't do that. You have too much to live for.'

'Then I wish I'd never woken up.'

TWELVE

I wake up to glitter against a midnight blue sky.

Faces above me. Dad, Eamon.

Sparks, floating, drifting, landing.

A glass of water at my lips.

'Let's get you home, champ.'

Dad's face is a white tablet against the dark of night.

'No.' My voice is raspy, throat dry.

I don't want to go home.

'I mean to the cabin,' Dad says.

'No.'

Can't he see?

'I'm not scared of fire.'

If I say it enough, it will be true.

Dad leans down, his rough skin at my ear. 'It's okay to be scared.'

'No.'

Dad brushes the hair off my face, helps me sit up.

There it is, the fire dragon, spitting, licking, twisting, curling.

'We didn't think,' Claudia whispers. 'I'm so sorry.'

'Paulie shouldn't have made it so big. He got carried away,' Opa says.

'I'm staying.'

I keep watching the flames. Don't dare take my eyes off them. My body shivers.

Claudia drapes a blanket over my shoulders. 'Okay, let's get you inside then.'

'No.'

'This isn't something you have to confront, champ.' Dad, soft in my ear.

'Why would you let me run now?'

They don't understand. I refuse to be scared of fire. Fire isn't like ugliness. It's not something I carry every day. Fire is the cause, but not the fear.

Eamon sits silently beside me. He's watching the flames too.

He saw me freak out. Nobody gets to see me freak out. I do it in bathroom stalls, locked away in my bedroom, in my secret space on the roof of our house, in the dark of my nightmares. Not in front of a bunch of people I barely know.

'I'll tell them to pile dirt on it, let it die down,' Opa says. 'That okay with you, Scarlett?'

I nod. So long as they don't rush me away like a scared little mouse. I need to tame the beast. Not run from it.

Opa and Claudia leave to sort out the fire. They start calling to people. Men and women begin shovelling dirt onto the flames.

The fire slowly shrinks.

'Sorry,' I say to Eamon.

'What for?'

'You know . . . fainting . . . freaking.'

He shrugs. 'I've seen worse.'

After a while, the fire is no longer wild and savage, just a smouldering pile of logs.

'I'm still sorry,' I say.

Dad and Eamon help me up.

'You're very lucky Eamon caught you when you fainted,' Dad says. 'You could have hurt yourself.'

I take a step towards the nearest wooden bench, but keep my eyes on the fire. Never again will I trust a naked flame. Still, I force myself to sit sandwiched between Dad and Eamon, watching the fire lick over the red embers.

The little kids seem to have disappeared. I've lost track of what time it is.

Claudia sits with the guitar again and starts singing softly in time with her strumming. So softly I can barely hear the words. All I catch is a sad longing in her voice.

Cat approaches us and takes Eamon by the hand, pulling at him.

'She wants me to put her to bed,' he says. 'Back in a sec.'

Eamon leaves just as Opa sits alongside Dad, and a wave of exhaustion washes over me. Panic attacks burn a lot of energy.

Dad starts asking Opa questions about the land, but I'm too tired to listen. I stare at the changing patterns in the small flames and yawn, leaning my head on Dad's shoulder. He pats my hair absent-mindedly.

'The caves in the hills, are they worth visiting?' Dad asks.

'Nah, we had to block access to them,' Opa says. 'Too many

people coming from all over to visit.'

'They must be pretty spectacular, then?'

'That's not why people were visiting. It was for the healing powers.'

'Healing powers?' I can hear a hint of mockery in Dad's voice, and I hope Opa doesn't pick up on it. Dad's never been one for superstition.

'The caves are made of limestone and the water that runs through them is dense in mineral deposits. There's a bit of science behind the benefits of trace minerals to the body, but not a lot of studies have been done on it. There are certain people though, naturopaths mostly, who swear by the healing power of minerals.'

'Like holy water, is it?' Dad says.

'They seem to think so. And I can't rule it out to be honest. I mean, none of us here ever seem to get sick. Whether it's the fresh air, the clean water or the high mineral intake, I couldn't tell you. All I can say is that while the rest of the world are getting flus and tummy bugs, we just don't. And when one of us gets injured, we don't seem to develop infections.'

'Maybe you need to start selling this magic water?' Dad jokes.

I sit up straight and Dad stops stroking my hair. Magic water. After all the time I've spent going to surgeons and doctors, using creams and ointments . . . it can't hurt. Nothing can hurt at this point.

'Actually, people did start selling our water. They came from all over, bottling up the stuff to sell at markets. But the limestone was being destroyed by the foot traffic. And the caves aren't stable. Crumbly when it's dry, slippery after a bluster. We don't even let the kids go anymore, so we figured why let hordes of visitors wander a space they don't understand? If it's not safe enough for our own kids, it's not safe enough for anyone. Only a matter of time before there'd be an accident. So we boarded up the road and blocked access. Every now and then determined folks still come on foot, but it's rare.'

By the time Eamon returns, the adults are dancing to the sound of Claudia's guitar, Dad doing his infamous goofy bear dance. The fire has been reduced to a pile of red rubble. It's almost dead, but I feel very much alive. No longer tired. I am owl-eyed, wide awake.

Eamon sits down next to me. He looks across to where Dad is dancing with Opa, and nods his head at them.

'Want to join the fools' club?'

I shake my head. I have other things on my mind.

'What are these caves I heard your opa talking to my dad about?'

'You mean the forbidden caves?' Eamon says.

'Are they the limestone ones?'

'Yeah. Nobody really visits them anymore.'

'Is it true the water has healing power?'

'Nah, that's just a myth.'

I look down at my hands. Of course. What am I, like six years old, to believe in magic water? What next, garden fairies? Heat rushes to my cheek and the harder I try not to look embarrassed, the hotter it burns.

The music changes, and the voice with it. I look over, thankful for the distraction.

‘Oh no, Opa’s taken the strings.’ Eamon drops his head in his hands.

But I keep watching. Not Opa. Dad. Whose hands are holding Claudia’s narrow waist. To the beat of Opa’s music, Claudia raises her arms above her head, ballerina-like, and Dad twirls her gently. Her patchwork skirt with its handkerchief hem flies out around her like a jagged star. Dad catches her when she’s facing him again, and, slowly, they dance. She, laughing at something he said and looking down at the ground. He, very much looking at her, holding her closer, their cheeks almost touching.

I haven’t seen this before. Dad, boxer, no-quitter, man of strength, suddenly looking soft and a bit shy with this woman in his arms. She, graceful, lithe, poised, as she spins and dances around him. Boxing is a type of dance, but not this type of dance.

I don’t know what I feel watching them. He’s the only man in my life. I’m the only girl in his. This should really sting. But there’s beauty in it. Symmetry.

‘They look good.’ Eamon, beside me. I’d almost forgotten he was there. Or that I was here. We’re all here, in this warped little paradise.

‘She’s very different, your mum.’

‘She’s beautiful, huh?’ He cocks his head to one side, watching her. ‘I reckon your dad might think so too.’ He grins, watching Dad’s goofy feet as he tries to impress Claudia. ‘I take it your mum’s not on the scene, then?’

‘She died when I was little.’

‘Oh, I’m sorry,’ Eamon says, looking away. ‘That’s tough.’

I shrug. ‘It’s not a big deal. I don’t even really remember her.’

'My dad may as well have died,' Eamon offers. 'I mean, he didn't—it's not the same thing, I know—just he may as well have. I don't even know where he is. Not that I miss him or anything.'

'Course not,' I say.

We can both sit here and lie to each other. Pretend it doesn't hurt to be missing a parent.

'So anyway, I could take you there if you want.'

'Where?'

'To the caves. If you wanna try the . . . healing water?'

Eamon looks me in the eye, a shadow of sadness hovering in his gaze. I look away.

Never, never do I want pity from this boy. 'Nah. Pretend I didn't even ask.'

Eamon's silent for a while. 'The caves are pretty awesome, you know. There's even a rock pool you can swim in. Like underground.'

I imagine submersing my whole body in the healing waters. Not just collecting a bit in a bottle, but swimming in it, drinking it, being inside it. I shake the thought away. Mineral water clearly isn't going to heal me, just like playing the If Only game about the day of the accident isn't going to undo what happened.

Then again, cave water isn't going to damage me either. And I've tried everything—every pill, potion and cream.

When I look back at Eamon, he's grinning wickedly.

'It's another of those adventures only for the wildly desperate or the wildly daring,' he says, raising one brow. 'Which one are you?'

This time, I'm not afraid to say it.

'I'm both. When can we go?'

I am up, dressed, ready and waiting before the sun has risen.

My heart is drumming as I leave Dad another note. He'll be happy that I'm getting out, especially after the fire last night. He doesn't need to know where I'm going. All he'll think is, *Good, Scarlett is mixing with kids again! Scarlett is returning to life!* He just has no idea what I'm actually facing today. How much bigger it is than this.

Swimming again. Baring my flesh. I think of Anna's pool party and shudder. But on Matilda Mountain, I feel very far away from parties. With Eamon, I might just be able to do it. Maybe.

I loop my towel around my neck, pull my hat down low over my forehead and ease the cabin door shut behind me. Then I wait, leaning against the balustrade of the verandah in the inky pre-dawn sky.

I half wish Eamon wasn't coming. But I can't find the caves without him.

The sky blanches white. The first kookaburra cackles. It's a warning that my hour of courage is getting nearer.

A faint humming noise finally sounds in the distance. I push off the verandah and peer in the direction of Eamon's place. My senses are sharp, my breath captive in my chest as I wait.

The humming grows slowly louder. Feminine, tuneless humming. Unmistakable Cat sounds.

My heart drops. It would be hard enough to swim with Eamon. But with Cat too?

On top of that, I didn't really want to share Eamon's attention. But then I crush my own thoughts, because it's not like Eamon's my boyfriend or anything. And Cat's only his sister. When did I get so possessive? It must be to do with seeing Dad and Claudia last night. They danced seven songs straight. A barefoot ballerina and a big dancing teddy bear. They would have danced longer if Claudia hadn't been coaxed back to the guitar. Even then, Dad sat opposite her the rest of the night, just staring. I wanted to slap him.

Today's not about that, though.

They break through the tree line at the same time, only they're not two, they're three.

Chief stops still when he sees the cabin, cocks his ears in my direction, frowning. The second he recognises me, he pelts full throttle towards me. The sun spills over the mountain, and he is a gold streak of lightning heading my way.

I brace against the cabin wall. He jumps up, one paw on each of my shoulders, licking my face from chin to ear and knocking off my hat. I'm laughing, but trying hard not to, trying to keep quiet so we don't wake Dad. By the time Eamon comes running over, I have managed to get Chief to sit down and to jam my hat back on. Chief leans against me, pushing me into the wall in his quest for a pat.

'Someone sure loves you,' Eamon whispers, giving him an ear rub. 'And I thought I'd be the one happiest to see you!'

My cheek burns. I focus on patting Chief's head, but Eamon's fingers brush mine accidentally as he scratches Chief's ear. He adjusts the towel around his neck.

'You ready?' he says. 'Got your swimmers?'

I lift the strap out from the neckline of my shirt as evidence. Pretend this is flippant. Like I swim in front of people every day.

'No water bottle? No backpack?' he teases.

I roll my eyes at him.

'Hope you don't mind me bringing Cat,' he says as we wait for her. 'She'd have cried all day if I left her behind again.'

'Of course. It's fine. Not like it's a date or anything.'

Eamon's ears are suddenly pink. 'Yeah, nothing like that.'

Then the thought hits me. Will I ever go on a date with a boy? Will anyone ever want to date a girl with scars like mine? I shake the thought away.

'Anyway, Cat won't tell anyone we snuck into the forbidden caves, will you, Cat?' he whispers as Cat reaches the cabin. 'Like Mum says, she keeps everyone's secrets.'

The forbidden caves are further than Tilly's Hut, but the trek is nowhere near as steep. Either side of us loom rock walls, stained and covered in lichen. Chief sniffs the stones ahead as we walk, and Cat follows, sometimes by Eamon's side, sometimes just behind him.

'I could take Cat all over the mountain in the space of a day and she wouldn't complain,' he says. 'So long as she's with me, she's a happy camper, right, Cat?'

Cat doesn't respond. But I get the feeling he's right.

Eamon has this aura about him that makes people want to

be near him. He's easy company. And even if he can be slightly annoying sometimes, he makes you feel like everything's okay.

'Here's where things get interesting,' he says. 'Cat, hold my hand.'

Cat doesn't volunteer her hand, but Eamon takes it anyway.

The ground dips down and becomes gritty under our feet. The trees thin and a ledge of rock drops away beneath us.

'Down this way,' Eamon says.

We walk through an arch of limestone, hollowed out by wind and rain. Chief trots ahead, following a narrow path carved into the ledge. The earth is damp, and he sniffs at mossy stones as the path leads us to an opening. Dark, like the mouth of a groper fish.

'Okay,' Eamon says. 'Forbidden caves at your service.'

It looks like the kind of place people go missing. The kind of gap in the earth that swallows people so completely they're never found again. A tomb carved into the rock.

'Is there air in there?' I ask.

'Plenty,' Eamon says.

'No nasty drops down deep cavernous holes?'

'Not where we're going.'

He steps through the mouth of the cave with Cat, into the darkness, and I follow. Cat suddenly shrieks and her voice bounces back at us.

'That's an excited shriek,' Eamon says. 'Not scared. Cat hasn't been to the caves in years, but her memory is incredible. She knows where we're going.'

From inside, I can see how the wind has hollowed out the walls of the cave. They're not smooth, though, they're mottled.

Along the edges of the cave, sharp jagged spikes point down from the roof and narrow spires of rock rise up to meet them, like teeth in a set of monster jaws. Sometimes the teeth touch, making columns.

Every so often, blades of light pierce the darkness from holes in the roof of the cave, spearing the floor with tiny spotlights shone onto invisible dancers. The walls glisten like they've been sprinkled with glitter, and a soft drippy sound echoes from somewhere deep in the cave.

'Wow,' I breathe.

'Cool, huh?' Eamon says. 'The stalactites and stalagmites have grown since I was last here.'

'The what?'

He gestures at the pointy teeth growing from the roof. 'Stalactites. They're the ones who hold on *tight* to the ceiling. And the stalagmites . . .' He points to the spires reaching up from the floor. 'They're hoping they *might* just reach the ceiling one day. Which one do you think you are, the kind who holds on tight or the kind who hopes they might?' He laughs to himself. 'I'm definitely the kind who hopes they might.'

I think for a moment. I was the kind who hopes they might in the *before*. But I'll never live in the *before* again.

'I think I might be the other kind,' I say quietly, reaching out to touch the gritty surface of one of the columns. 'How long do you think these take to form?'

Eamon shrugs. 'Hundreds of years, they say. Maybe even a thousand.'

'Wow. It's only been five hundred and seventeen days since

I had my accident. That's not much more than one year. It feels silly to be counting the days of my scars when these caves were here hundreds of years before I was born and will probably be here hundreds of years after I die too. Our time on earth is so short, really, isn't it?'

'Mum says our time here is equivalent to one breath of the universe.'

Chief barks at the entrance to the cave and his bark is magnified, repeating back at us. Eamon whistles to Chief, who whines and paws at the ground. His shadow is blocking the light at the mouth of the cave. One more whistle from Eamon, and Chief bounds clumsily in. He turns back and barks at the cave entrance, his hackles up, before running full pelt into Eamon's legs.

'Tell you what, boy, for such a mean-looking dog, you really are a sook,' Eamon says, patting Chief on the flank.

'How far does the cave go?' I say.

'You'd be surprised. The way I remember it, they go quite a way under the mountain, but we shouldn't need to go that far to reach the water. Depends how much rain we've had. But don't worry, it only gets dangerous after a storm—that's when the water pours down the mountain into the caves. Let's head down and see what level the water's at.'

We stay close to the right-hand side of the cave, where the limestone has made a natural ledge along the floor of the cave. The tiptoe of our footsteps echoes in the dusky light. To our left, the ground is covered in dimpled, uneven rocks that drop away into deep chasms.

As we head further into the cave, I trace my fingertips along its cool waxen wall. A wall which isn't smooth or perfect, but rutted and scarred from its hundreds of years of existence. Yet still somehow breathtaking. There are holes in the rock overhead where patches of sunshine filter through, but the further we go, the more the ceiling closes over.

We walk until the air becomes cooler and then we can walk no further, because our path is blocked by water. A natural rock pool, bathed in a shard of light from a lone crack in the cave wall. And filling the rock pool is exactly what I've come here for. Mineral water the colour of jade washes gently against the ledge we're standing on. Water plinks softly from the ceiling into the pool, sending little ripples across the surface.

Cat squeals and her voice is shrill in its echo. She strips off her clothes without hesitation, and I watch as her tall, slim, unblemished body leaps into the water.

'Can she swim?' I ask suddenly.

'Can she ever,' Eamon says. 'Try getting her out. That's when we'll have problems!'

Cat pays no attention to me or Eamon or even Chief, who is whining for her at the edge of the pool and pawing at the water. Envy stabs me in the heart. I wish so much that I could care as little as her.

I'm aware of Eamon stripping off his shirt beside me and kicking off his shoes. Another unblemished body, lean and pale in the half light.

'Here goes nothing,' he says, and he plunges into the water with a big splash, disappearing beneath the surface. When he bursts back up, he's gasping.

'It's absolutely freezing!' He treads water. 'I tell you what . . .' His breaths are sharp. 'If I was game enough . . . you'd better not . . . chicken out!'

It's time to do it. Peel off the dressing of my clothes and show him what I look like underneath. But my fingers are frozen. I can't move them. My heart hits hard against my ribs and my armpit feels suddenly sweaty.

It's not the cold water I care about. Let it freeze over me. It's Anna's pool party I'm thinking of. The girls with their smooth sun-kissed bodies, just like Cat's. The selfies, the filters, the perfection of it all.

But this is the healing water I need. So why am I frozen?

AFTER

I am frozen inside my body.

They tell me my muscles will grow stronger with exercise, but it takes me two hours to feed myself lunch.

I would rather not eat at all. Or lift my fingers to my mouth, a fork to my lips.

It takes too long to form the right sounds to make one word, two words, three. I don't have the energy for a full sentence.

Baby words: wee, no, Dad. I'd rather not speak at all.

Everywhere, everything is pain.

Life is finding a thousand tiny ways to torture me.

I hate physios.

I hate doctors.

I hate nurses.

I hate needles.

I hate dressings.

I hate infections.

I hate scars.

I hate life.

I have never been so hateful.
Hateful, helpless, ugly.

THIRTEEN

'You look ugly when you cry,' Gran said when I was little. 'So much prettier when you smile.'

She meant to make me stop crying. Instead, I just learnt not to cry around *her*. Smile through my pain. Pretty was more important than sad or angry or hurt. Always be pretty.

I know Gran didn't mean it like that, she just didn't understand the power of her words. Like her parents before her, I guess, who put her in the beauty pageants. When she was young, Gran didn't have a choice, and by the time she did, she'd learnt that being pretty won her love from her parents, from the world. She was taking out local pageants, then state ones, and before she knew it, the Miss World beauty pageant was upon her. Without being pretty, without being perfect, none of that glory was possible.

For me, it was just seconds between pretty and ugly. Prettiness was a gift freely given to me by life, then freely taken away.

Gran has never seen me cry since the accident. She never will see me cry. I can't seem to give her my tears; it requires a level of trust we've never had. But sometimes I wonder how someone like my dad was made inside someone like her. Dad, who doesn't care about faces or scars, except for the stories they tell.

Now I am standing at the edge of the water, my knees trembling. And stripping down to my swimmers feels a bit like crying in front of Gran. I can hear her voice. *So much prettier when you smile.* My body is so much prettier with its clothes on, covering up its painful story. But why is it even my job to be pretty? Why can't I just be?

'Hey,' Eamon says softly. He pulls himself out of the water, shivering from cold as much as I am trembling from fear.

He wraps an icy arm around my shoulder. 'Cold, aren't I?'

I nod, trying to paste on the smile I save for Gran, but it doesn't work with Eamon.

'You know I don't . . . give a toss what you look like?' His teeth are chattering hard. 'And Cat?' He looks across at her, floating on her back, mesmerised by the stalactites pointing like spears down towards the water. 'She won't . . . even look at you.'

'It *is* healing water, right?'

'Well, Cat looks pretty . . . chill in it . . . so it must be.' His chest rises and falls with each gasp of air. 'You've just gotta be like . . . that girl in Tilly's story. Stand on the edge . . . and take a flying leap.'

'Um, you know she didn't really fly like a bird, right? She leapt to her death.'

Eamon studies me for a long time, his teeth chattering. 'No, I don't . . . think so.'

'Yeah she did. I know I said I didn't want the story to end with her dying, but you have to face facts. She died. Just like

Tilly's daughter. The bird thing was a metaphor for her death.'

'Nope . . . Don't believe it . . . She was taking a chance.' Eamon's body is quaking violently alongside me now, his lips tinged purple. 'Now, look . . . I'm getting hypothermia.'

I take in the cave in the dim light, jade water splashing up against the ledge, Cat looking like a perfect mermaid on the set of an animated film. I would be the sea monster.

But there are no cameras to take my photo, nobody snapping pictures for social media. Not even direct sunlight to highlight my three-dimensional scars. If I can't swim in healing water in the privacy of a cave, I'll never be able to swim anywhere again. I grit my teeth.

'Okay, I'm going in,' I say.

'Okay.' Eamon steps back and extends a shaky arm. 'Ladies first . . . courage first.'

He has no idea how much courage this takes.

I do it fast, the same way the nurses would change my dressings. Strip them off. Get it over with. I lay down my towel, followed by my shorts. Now for the hard part. I take off my hat, resting it on my towel, and, finally, lift my shirt.

The skin on my arms is thick and patterned, a latticework of scars that extends across my chest and up my neck. But my one-piece swimmers hide my tummy at least.

I leap.

It's not courage but fear that gets me in that water, shrieking from the shock of the icy pins against my skin. I draw small gasps of air into my lungs.

'Told you . . . it was cold,' Eamon laughs. Then he presses

himself back against the wall of the cave. 'Okay, my turn,' he says.

He takes a small run up and leaps into the pool. He disappears beneath the water, then bursts back through the surface, gulping for air. 'The things . . . I do for you!'

The arctic water cramps up my hands and presses in painfully around my body, but if this is healing, then give me pain. Pain doesn't frighten me anymore.

I kick my legs to get the blood flowing and do a few froggy strokes. Put my head under and gulp great mouthfuls of water. I want to be healed inside *and* outside—all over.

Eamon comes after me with big graceful strokes. If Cat is the mermaid, he is the merman. Water must be a big part of their lives on the mountain.

'You're very . . . at home here,' I say, gasping from the cold.

'A water baby . . . Born in the water . . . born a fish, Mum says.'

'How do you get . . . born in the water?' My arms begin to ache. Freeze.

'Homebirth . . . of course.'

I laugh. 'Of course. I was . . . born in a hospital . . . but you were probably . . . born in a stream or something.'

He shakes his head. 'Blow-up pool . . . outside the village hall.'

'Where we ate?' I say.

'Yep. Born at night under . . . the sign of Pisces, the sign of the fish . . . been of the water ever since . . . Can't live without it.'

I laugh. 'You'd struggle . . . in the city then.'

'Yeah, I'm not made . . . for the city. I need . . . water on my skin the way . . . I need air in my lungs.' He dives deep under the water and bursts through the surface again a moment later. 'Meet Fish Boy!'

Chief crouches down on his front paws and barks at Eamon, his ears cocked. I laugh, and the sound that echoes back at me from the walls of the cave is unfamiliar.

'I thought you *caught* fish . . . didn't know you were one,' I tease.

'In the water, I'm the fish . . . on land, I'm the fisherman,' he says. 'And our next stop on this tour . . . is my favourite fishing spot.'

Cat laps the edge of the rock pool and Chief follows her. If Eamon is a fish and Cat is a mermaid, what am I? Here in the cave, I don't feel like a monster. I feel like a girl. A girl on a wild adventure.

We swim until our muscles lock up from the cold and we can no longer feel our feet. We swim until the water is bitter and the pain is great. When I can't stand it another second, I pull myself out of the pool and to my towel, dripping and shaking, my skin tight and zinging and alive.

But for Eamon, it's not so easy.

'Cat, it's time,' he says.

She ignores him, frolicking in the water and pretending not to hear.

'Cat, time to go!'

He reaches for her hand, but she swims away from him. He laughs. Looks at me.

'Told you so,' he says, flicking droplets from his hair. 'Once you get her in the water, good luck getting her out.'

I bite my towel to stop my teeth chattering as I watch him chase Cat around the pool.

'Gotcha,' he says, and she moans. 'Time to come in now, Cat. We've gotta catch ourselves some fish for dinner.'

The second he has her, she goes limp, making him drag her through the water to the edge of the pool.

'She's a bugger,' he says. Turning to her, 'Don't help me at all, will you, huh?'

Cat just floats on her back as he pulls her along, a small smile on her lips.

I smile too, as a bubble of hope rises in my chest. Maybe this special mountain, this healing water, could be the very thing to fix me. Opa said the caves are dangerous, but they feel like the safest place I've been in a very long time.

Sunshine bites at my eyes as we step out into the middle of a warm, bright day, my towel slung over my shoulder. I feel like I'm still floating in the water as we follow the trail back in the direction of the cabin.

We reach the stream that runs below the house, and a fallen old log tangled with wild vines and covered in moss makes us a bridge across to the far bank. Eamon takes Cat by the hand to help her up and they begin to cross. Chief follows Eamon, pawing his way onto the log, but slips off and lands with a splash in the stream. As Chief swims and bounds through the water, I balance my hands out either side of me and follow Eamon onto the log.

My feet are light and sure, and it feels almost like I'm dancing, dancing for me. So halfway along the log, I do a double pirouette.

'Whoa, do that again.'

I look up. Eamon is already on the other side of the stream, watching me.

'No,' I say.

'Go on, show me. Show me that trick!'

'I'm not dancing for you.'

'Call it spinning, then. Spin like that again, or will you fall?' he teases.

'Never,' I say.

And I take a couple of steps forward, pirouetting once, just to show him, before dismounting from the log.

'I say you're wildly daring,' he says. 'Not desperate. First the leap into sub-zero cave water, now your funky moves on the log.'

'I'll settle for plain old wild,' I say. Because today, I don't feel desperate *or* daring. Just wild. Alive.

We follow the stream down along its bank. Cat walks with Chief ahead of us, and Eamon is quiet for a while. He looks at me, then looks away. I pull my hat down lower over my face.

'You said dancing's about beauty and grace, right?'

'It is.'

'And you think you don't have that anymore.'

'You don't know what I think.'

We walk the rest of the way in silence. Who is he to tell me what I think? He's never danced a day in his life, I bet. He has no idea what it takes. Or what's expected.

We reach a part of the stream where a willow drips its heavy boughs into the water. I recognise the tree. The bend in the stream. I look across to the other side of the bank, expecting to see my dancing deer, but she's not there. I don't even know for certain whether the deer *was* a she, but she had a special grace about her that made me believe she was.

'*This* is your favourite fishing spot?'

'Yep. You found it on your very first day.'

'Well, this is a disappointment. I thought you were taking us somewhere special.'

Eamon smiles, and sunlight pours into his eyes, highlighting flecks of yellow and green. 'Oh, but this is special. Come and see.'

Eamon swings up into the willow's branches like a monkey, and disappears in a crop of leaves. He expects that I can climb in the same way he can. He doesn't know how many weeks of physio it has taken for me to get this much strength back in my arms. And I love that.

So I pull myself after him, wincing against the burn in my arms. Some days it feels like my arms are painted on. I don't trust their strength, their ability to hold weight the way they should or to pull me along the way they used to. Some days they feel fragile, like they'll tear in half and never work again.

Today isn't one of those days. And Dad would tell me to climb this tree, swim in that cave. Especially since I skipped our boxing session this morning. So I haul myself up to the next branch, laughing as a twig catches a loop of my hair and makes it stick out beneath my hat.

Eamon is sitting on the limb of a thick overhanging branch, his legs dangling.

'Find a perch,' he says.

Dangling alongside Eamon is a bucket, which is tied to a branch above him. He reaches into the bucket and pulls out a circular hand reel with a hook on the end of it. He hands it to me and grabs one for himself, then pulls a bag of bread out of the bucket.

'Bream will eat pretty much anything, and they like shady spots. Which is why this one's a winner.'

He shows me how to roll the bread into a ball and thread it on the hook, then we both throw out our lines.

'Now hold it and wait. Don't yank at it if you feel a nibble, you need to let him get a good bite first.'

I rest a finger against my fishing line. Cat swings from the lower branches of the willow tree, and Chief lies down to rest in the shade.

'So what do you need to be a fisherman?' I ask Eamon.

'Not much. Just a reel, a hook, some bait and a bit of patience.'

'And what would you do if someone took away your hook?'

Eamon looks at me, frowning. 'I'd get another one.'

'What if you couldn't?'

'What do you mean? I'd go home and get another packet.'

'What if there were no other packets anywhere? What if you could never again find a hook?'

'I don't get it.'

'You say I should dance, but you don't understand what's been taken from me. You need the right tools.'

We sit in silence, watching the water swirling slowly downstream.

'Look, I don't know who you were before, or much about you at all really. But nobody took your legs or arms.'

'My arms.'

I lift my sleeve so he can see the extent of the scarring. This time in the sunlight. Thick and multicoloured.

'Yeah, but that's just your skin.'

'It's *not* just my skin.' But I stop from saying too much more because I don't want him to know how weak I really am. I want to be the wildly daring girl he thinks I am. Not the fragile weak one I am in my other life. I don't want him to treat me like I can't do everything he can.

'There's also the small matter of my . . .' I make a sweeping gesture around my face. 'It's not easy getting around in this outfit.'

'But that outfit's your skin. You're still kinda beautiful.'

Only if you squint. 'Don't lie to me.'

'I don't lie.'

'Nothing about this is beautiful.' I jam my hat down over my eyes so that I can barely see. 'Nothing.'

'Beautiful is different to being pretty. You know that, right?'

'Wow, now there's a new line. Beautiful, pretty, it all means the same thing. Trust me, I've looked it up.'

'It's not the same at all,' he says. 'Pretty is just for looking at.'

'And beautiful isn't?'

'No. Like, I think my mum's beautiful, even though she's old.'

'Yeah, she totally is.'

'And see that gnarled old gum tree over there?' He points at the giant tree on the far bank, its bleached white trunk dripping with rusty colours. 'Don't you think that's beautiful?'

'Yeah, of course, but—'

'And the caves are beautiful, even though they're crumbling. And Tilly's Hut, that's beautiful, even though it's ancient, and storms have their own kind of beauty, even though they can be scary. And oysters, they're all kinds of knobbly shapes, but they keep beautiful pearls inside them.'

'Yeah, well, that's nature. Nature's allowed to be different. Nobody expects nature to be perfect.'

He laughs. 'And humans aren't part of nature? Is that what they teach you in the city?'

'No. They teach us how to manipulate nature.'

'Of course. Take all the beauty from it, make everyone and everything look the same, right?'

I think of my white-picket-fenced street with its rows of neat, rendered houses.

'But see, you're kinda beautiful in ways you probably don't see. Like how your eyes go rainbow-shaped when you laugh. Or the way you dance when you don't know anyone's watching.'

'Don't talk about that. I wanted to die.'

'And your scars. I know you don't like them, but I think they're kinda cool.'

'Scars are not cool.'

'They are. Scars are strong, and I'd choose strong over plain old pretty any day. Scars show the world you went through something terrible and survived. Everyone knows that being brave is beautiful, but not everyone gets to be brave, because not everyone has your story.'

'And what is my story? Tell me.'

He shrugs. 'That's up to you. You're the only person who gets to tell it. Like I'm the only person who gets to tell my story.'

'I want my old story.'

'You don't get it, do you? The old one doesn't matter anymore. Whatever you were before, it's finished.'

I draw a sharp breath. His words are painful. I don't want to hear them. Can't accept them. Pretty Scarlett, gorgeous Scarlett, perfect Scarlett. She can't be finished. I'm still looking for her, still hunting for ways to bring her back. But Eamon goes on anyway.

'This has happened to you now. It's like with Cat. Mum was devastated when the doctors told her Cat had an intellectual disability and would be non-verbal for life. Cried every time Cat had a birthday. But it didn't change anything. Cat was born with autistic spectrum disorder. This happened. And even if we *could* change it, make Cat a regular eleven-year-old, she wouldn't be her . . . and Cat's my favourite.'

He looks down at her, swinging from the branch, singing to herself. 'I love her the most. I love her even more because of how she is. She hasn't got a mean word to say or a mean thought to think, and you can't say that about many people. And you—you have scars, sure, but they make you different. And different isn't bad, it's interesting. The fire, it's part of your story. But not your whole story. Just the beginning of it. You kinda need to accept that. Maybe even be grateful for what it's taught you.'

'Well, that's easy to say when you're perfect.'

I don't want to accept what happened to me. Prettiness shouldn't be lost. One burn, one accident, one wrong step. I'd go back and undo it in a second. I'll always want to undo it, no matter how much time passes. Go back to the perfect I never knew I was before.

But I don't get a second chance at those moments that changed me. I get one life, and that's going to be a life where I'm scarred and different. I won't live to be hundreds or thousands of years old like the caves. Maybe I'll get sixty more years. Should I use them chasing the kind of perfect I'll never catch?

There are still things I *can* catch, of course. The thrill of icy water against my skin, the warmth of summer sun kissing my face, the glory of stars from my special place on the roof, the shivery feeling of that first brush stroke on a blank canvas. No burn can take those things away.

'Did you just say I'm perfect?' Eamon grins, his ears flushed.

'What? No, I meant—'

'Yeah, you did. You said I'm perfect.'

He's going to milk this. I can already feel the blood pumping to my cheek as I try to backpedal.

'No, I meant unblemished, unscarred—whoa!' The reel jumps in my hand.

'Hold onto it,' Eamon says. 'Don't yank too hard, you've got one!'

The line is tugged again.

'Looks like a big one too,' he says, shuffling closer. 'Let him go for a bit.'

The line jerks and stretches, fishing wire flicking over my fingers and off my reel. The strength of the pull makes me wobble.

Eamon holds my shoulders to steady me.

'Stop the line now,' he says, putting his finger on the reel to stop the runaway fishing wire. 'Let him go, let him go . . . Now reel him in slowly, wrap the line around . . . that's it! That's it, you're doing it!'

I bite my bottom lip as I listen to Eamon, and slowly, slowly, force the fishing line around the reel. My heart is thundering with anticipation. I've never caught a fish before.

Eamon helps me wind it in when the line gets too tight, until suddenly, through the water, a silver flicker, a dazzling flash and a gaping mouth breaks through the surface.

'Keep winding,' Eamon says.

I wind the reel, until there is a fish dangling in the air on the bottom of my line, flicking its tail and arching its body.

'Ladies and gentlemen,' Eamon announces, 'the catch of the day, right here!'

He doubles himself over in a bow to an invisible audience.

We reel the fish up until we're holding its soft silvery body in our hands. Scales shimmer in the sun, reflecting rainbows. It's the magic fish from my childhood books. The magic fish from the magic water of our magic mountain.

Dad barbecues some veggies to go with the fish for dinner.

As we sit down by the wood fire to eat, he says, 'I still can't believe you caught a fish. And I didn't even get to show you how!'

'Oh, don't worry, I was taught by a mountain boy,' I say flippantly. 'He knows all the tricks.'

I might be being a bit mean. But I blame that stabbing feeling in my chest as I watched Dad with Claudia last night. He needs to know what that feels like.

Dad only laughs. 'He's a kid, champ. I think I have a few more years of fishing under my belt than he does.'

'Very funny, Dad. But I doubt it. He fishes, like, every day.'

'Does he just? Well, I think I might need to show you what I can do with a lure and a fishing rod, then. If he's so wonderful, we might need to have ourselves a little fish off. It'll be our thing.'

'Our thing?' I smile. Dad thinks he's still cool.

'Yeah, our thing. You brought home one fish with Eamon. Let's see how many you and I can reel in. Deal?'

'Deal.'

I look sideways at him, grey creeping up his hairline, his stubble growing out a bit rough, his face creased in all the right ways. My name inked on his arm. On his heart. Maybe he *is* still cool in his own way. In a dad kind of way. A *my* dad kind of way.

'Something kinda happened today,' I say.

'What?' Dad sounds wary.

'It's hard to explain, but I started to feel like maybe things will work out somehow.'

He stops eating. Puts down his fork. Blinks hard a few times, his eyes gathering water.

'Course they will. You're stronger than any fighter I've met, champ. And I'd never let things *not* work out.' I think of all the times I wanted Dad to throw in the towel for me, let me give up . . . but he wouldn't. I thought he was being cruel, but maybe he was just not letting me give up on myself.

'I know my wounds will never heal to what they were before,

but maybe one day I'll be okay with that.'

Dad smiles softly. 'Champ, what you gotta understand is that you don't *have* wounds anymore. You have scars, and scars are healings. They're where the tissue grew strong to cover your wounds.'

AFTER

'It's to cover your wounds.'

The suit is thick and tight and crushing.

'Try it on for size.'

There are holes for my nose, holes for my eyes, a hole for my mouth.

It's a Halloween costume.

'How long do I have to wear it?'

'You can take it off one hour of every day.'

'One hour?'

'Once we get it made up, you'll need to wear it twenty-three hours a day for the next twelve months. It will help smooth your scars. Improve the outcome.'

That's what I am now: an outcome.

I hate the suit.

I hate the tight, unable-to-breathe feeling of it.

I hate that I look like a seal in a balaclava.

I hate my scars most of all.

Scars are not made for dancing.

FOURTEEN

I am dancing. Across an ivy-twined beam on stage. I move into fourth position, leap like a deer, arms outstretched. Do a plié, a double pirouette.

I spin and leap and stretch and twist across the beam.

My bare arms are graceful as they rise and fall. A medley of scars.

My body is not on fire, only my heart. And it beats with fury as I bow to the blackened crowd.

Clapping. The crowd starts clapping.

Someone stands, illuminated.

'Whoa, do that again,' he says.

I jolt awake. Not screaming, just my heart beating like wings in my chest.

I get up and start breakfast. Toast and scrambled eggs, sliced avocado and tomatoes. A champion's breakfast. I carry it into Dad's bedroom on a wooden tray with two cups of tea. He makes a hunched lump beneath the crocheted blanket, curled up facing the window.

I put the tray down on Dad's bedside table, sit on the edge of his bed and give him a gentle nudge on the shoulder.

'Wakey, wakey.'

He rolls over, a hand over his eyes. But when he sees me, he sits bolt upright in his singlet.

'What's wrong?'

Dad suffers from the same condition as me. What Nikki calls 'worst first thinking'. She says after you've been through a trauma, you live on the edge of catastrophe. Always expecting another disaster.

'Nothing's wrong,' I say.

Dad rubs his bleary morning face. 'Geez, you scared me.'

'I just made you breakfast.'

Dad wriggles over to make room for me and I bring the breakfast tray across.

'Well, doesn't this look amazing?' he says. 'You'd better be careful, I might start to get used to room service.'

We eat side by side on Dad's bed as the morning sun spills in through his curtains, setting the small room ablaze.

'You're gonna miss this place when we leave, aren't you?' he says.

'Yep. Saggy beds, wonky floors and gappy walls. I'll miss it all.'

'Don't worry, champ, we'll come back. I'm actually falling a little bit in love with the place myself.'

I stiffen at the word 'love'.

'I know why you want to come back.' I look at him sideways.

'Oh yeah, Miss Smarty Pants? Why?'

'A certain dancer with a long braid and a flowy dress.'

Dad smiles and his whole face lights up. 'Claudia's an amazing woman. But just because I danced with a woman, doesn't mean

I'm dating her, champ. It's just nice to be in female company sometimes. Men and women can be friends, you know. Like you and Eamon, right?'

He has a point. I'd hate him to make out something was happening between me and Eamon just because we like to hang out.

'So we'll mark this place on the map?' I say.

Dad and I have a map on his bedroom wall at home, where we put a star on all the places we visit that are worth returning to.

'Definitely map worthy,' Dad says. 'We'll be marking it.' He looks down at his bare arm alongside mine. 'Speaking of maps, between my ink and your scars, our arms are quite the roadmap, aren't they?'

My arm is narrow and lacquered shiny with scar tissue, his is thick and coloured with names, boxing gloves, numbers.

'Just like the map on my wall, we should always be proud of where we've been.'

I know it makes sense, what he's saying. And I can nod along. I *do* nod along. I just wish I fully believed it.

I don't have a single nightmare the second week. I sleep all night, every night, without waking. Without dreams. It's the deep sleep of the well-rested.

Each morning, Dad and I get up early for our boxing session. Eamon has started joining us. I laugh at his style. Arms loose, guard poor, not protecting his cheeks, Dad getting in a few good body shots. But Eamon's keen to learn, so he keeps coming back for more punishment.

This morning, Dad told Eamon to invite his family over for dinner. I raised an eyebrow at Dad, which he ignored. He is so obvious. Eamon said Claudia would love that, nobody ever cooks for her. So they're coming at six.

Anyone would think we had a master chef coming to judge dinner. Dad spends all afternoon sorting out the ingredients: chopping the basil, the garlic, the ginger, squeezing lemon juice into a bowl, marinating the fish, chopping the veggies, drizzling olive oil and garlic over them.

When we hear Chief barking in the crisp evening air, Dad says, 'They really did bring the whole family.'

I go out to greet them on the deck, and they emerge along the track from the twilight. As they get nearer, I see that Eamon has tidied his hair, Cat's braids are tight and Claudia is wearing a turquoise dress, jewelled with gemstones. It trails behind her as she walks. Her hair isn't braided, but falls long and wavy to her elbows. If mother nature were a goddess, she would look like this.

Chief comes running when he sees me, and gives me his trademark slam against the side of the cabin, licking my face. Claudia gasps.

'Chief! Oh, sweetie, I'm so sorry. We need to teach that dog some manners!'

I laugh. 'It's okay, I'm used to it.'

When Dad opens the front door to greet everyone, I notice he's changed into his nice denim shorts. Gone is the holey t-shirt from earlier, and in its place is a collared button-up one with short sleeves rolled up to show off his biceps. And his tattoos, which are on full display.

But Cat doesn't care how he looks. She walks straight past him and into the cabin like she owns the place. Which I guess she technically does. Dad's not fussed, though. It's not Cat he dressed up for.

Dad and Claudia stand awkwardly at the door a moment.

'You look amazing,' Dad says.

'Thank you,' Claudia says. 'And here's a little something from us.' She hands Dad a hamper of nuts, bread, olives and cheese.

Chief follows us all inside, and Dad doesn't question the fact that a horse-sized dog is standing in our living room. Cat spins around next to him, hands out either side of her, and Dad lights the wood fire as dusk settles over the cabin. He cracks open a bottle of red wine, pours a couple of glasses and offers one to Claudia as Cat takes off down the hall.

'Cat!' Claudia says. 'Eamon, can you . . .'

'I'll get her.'

'Let her go, it's fine,' Dad says.

Eamon and I follow Cat to my room. She's running her fingers along the palette of watercolour paint that's sitting on my bedside table. That gives me an idea. I grab my thick sheets of absorbent paper, the paints and brushes. I set up at the dining table and as Cat watches, I fill a glass with water and open the paints. She squeals.

'Someone's excited,' Eamon says.

He helps her hold the brush and we teach her how to dip it into the water, then the paint and blot it onto the page.

She quickly grabs hold of the idea and fills sheet after sheet with colour. She doesn't tire of it, even when the colours start to mix.

Dad and Claudia move outside to the deck, where they sit on a wooden bench seat under the amber glow of the porchlight and watch the dying light of the day drain from the sky. Every so often, I steal a glance at them. It's weird seeing Dad with a woman. The way his face comes alive. The attention he pays her. I notice Eamon watching too.

'This is bizarre,' he says. 'Our parents are on a date.'

We laugh.

I hear snippets of their conversation, but Claudia's voice is soft and difficult to hold onto. From what I can gather, she's telling Dad about how she came to live on the mountain.

'I was pregnant with Cat and feeling a bit abandoned by the world,' she says wistfully. 'Until the mountain claimed me, and I've never looked back since. What about you? How did you end up in the city?'

Dad takes a long sip of wine. Then I hear him mention her name. Astrid. He still chokes up when he says it, even though it's been long enough for me to have only one memory of her. But he has lots of memories. Their love didn't die, only she did. He talks about Gran too. Dad isn't as quiet as Claudia, so whether he means for me to or not, I hear everything.

'She can be tough, old-fashioned, downright grouchy sometimes. But she does her best with my kids. She never complains. She's not meant to still be raising kids, not at her age. And you know, since the accident with Scarlett, Ma takes her to every doctor's appointment, every physio session. She was there for every surgery. She carries a lot of guilt about being the driver, even though it was the truckie who was charged. Dangerous driving resulting in grievous bodily harm. He could have killed them both. He very nearly did kill Scarlett. For a while there, we thought she wouldn't pull through.'

I've never thought about how Gran could have died in the accident. Or how I might have felt if she did. Would I have spent the last seventeen months blaming her if she'd died in that blaze? I've blamed her just because she was there, she was driving. Not because it was actually her fault.

Claudia sips delicately from her wine. 'That must have been tough.'

'Yeah, it was. But I'm pretty sure you've dealt with your own tough things. And being a parent on your own, it's not easy. I know that much. Which is why it's been great to get away from life for a bit. Even if the cabin's a bit old and leaky and the power goes out from time to time,' he jokes.

Claudia laughs. 'You know, I helped build this "old" cabin.'

'Oh man.' Dad presses his fingers to his eyes. 'Now, don't I feel terrible. I didn't mean . . .'

'It's fine! It's as imperfect as the rest of us. Eamon's Opa built most of it. We never meant it to be a world famous monument.'

'Well,' Dad says, 'it's a fine cabin.'

Claudia just laughs. 'It's okay, really. We all know it's wonky. Actually, the village rarely has anything to do with the city folk who stay in the cabin. Most times they expect things to be a little too perfect, you know? So usually we prefer to keep our distance. But I'm very glad we didn't keep our distance this time.'

'So am I,' Dad says. 'Like you wouldn't believe.'

Ugh, I want to cringe for him. *Stop it, Dad!*

Eamon just smiles at me. 'He's got it bad, your dad.'

'Tell me about it.'

But then I hear Claudia's voice. 'It almost feels like . . . we were meant to meet. The kids get on so well. All of them.'

I look at Eamon. He holds his hands up in surrender. They both have it bad.

By the time Dad comes back inside, I've packed up the paints and washed the brushes and a string of Cat's paintings are drying on the kitchen bench. I want to pull Dad down the hallway and tell him to cool it with Claudia. Not because I don't like her, but because the man is embarrassing me. He totally needs to dial it back. Except Dad's busy looking for the fish he spent all afternoon marinating.

'Scarlett . . .' he calls. 'Any idea where the fillets went?'

'Nope.'

'They were right here,' Dad says.

Chief cringes and drops his head in his spot beneath the benchtop. He's licking his paws, a long shred of basil hanging from his lips.

Eamon gets to his feet. 'Chief, you didn't!'

Oh, but it's clear that Chief very much did. When we bend down to investigate, we can even smell the garlic and ginger on his breath.

'All of them?' Dad says, and the despair is plain in his voice.

'Well, he's a sixty-kilo dog,' Eamon says. 'So I think the answer is probably yes.'

'Oh, this is a disaster.'

Claudia floats in during the midst of the so-called disaster, but only laughs when she hears what's happened.

'This is no crisis,' she says. 'What else do we have? When you live on a mountain, you get quite good at improvising.'

'I've made up a stack of veggies,' Dad says, 'but the fish was the best part.'

'Hey, we love veggies, don't we, Eam? We eat fish so often, but very rarely does anyone bake us veggies.'

I see Dad's shoulders relax. 'Veggies it is then.'

Claudia ties Chief up and suggests we eat under the stars, so Dad grabs a blanket and spreads it out beneath the chandelier of celestial light above us.

We sit cross-legged in a circle, eating with just a fork, admiring the abundance of stars visible in the moonless night.

'These are my favourite kind of lights,' Claudia says. 'They never burn out or need replacing. And they don't use coal.'

When dinner is finished, Dad and I clear everyone's plates, then we all lie on our backs and stargaze. It reminds me of my place on the roof at home, but this is a happy kind of stargazing. Not lonesome. Eamon shows me the scorpion with its flicky tail, and points out Mars, which is the reddest star in the sky.

Claudia begins to sing, and Eamon joins her. Most of their songs we don't know, so they throw in some old classics like *YMCA* so that we can sing along. Dad sounds terrible, but none of us care. It's not like there's anybody else to hear us.

The night wears on, and Cat starts whining.

'Well, little miss is getting tired, so we'd better head off before she melts down,' Claudia says. 'Thank you for—'

'We'll walk you home,' Dad says. 'Won't we, Scarlett?'

'Of course we will, *Dad*,' I say, emphasising the word 'Dad'.

Are all men this gaga?

Eamon and I trail behind with Chief and Cat, planning our next fishing expedition, as Dad and Claudia walk ahead of us. I watch their fingers brush from time to time. When we get to the caravan, I follow Eamon inside. He gets me a drink of water and hands Cat her pyjamas to change into.

Outside the door, we can hear Dad saying goodbye to Claudia.

'Well, I had an amazing night,' he says. 'Even with the dog eating the dinner I spent all day preparing.'

Claudia laughs. 'Sorry about that. But it was lovely. Thank you.'

Eamon bites his bottom lip to stop from laughing.

'They are such a cliché,' I whisper.

'Tell me he's not about to go in for a kiss.'

I grimace. 'I don't even want to know.'

In the short silence that follows, Eamon and I raise our eyebrows at each other.

'Awkward!' I whisper.

'Okay, Scarlett,' Dad calls. 'We need to let these good people get to bed.'

'Alright, night, Eamon,' I say.

He gives me a one-armed hug and whispers in my ear, 'We just survived their first date.'

I laugh.

When I pass Claudia, there's a small smile playing on her lips.

Do they think we don't know?

On the walk home, Dad whistles a tune of his own making.

'It would be an interesting way of life out here, champ, wouldn't it?'

'Uh-huh. As I said from the beginning.'

'So much more of a sense of community than in the city. The people are kind of incredible too, aren't they?'

'I think you're talking about just one person, Dad. You don't seem to have spent a huge amount of time talking to anyone else.'

'Well, she is a bit of a shining star. Even you can see it, champ, I know you can.'

'Maybe we should move here after all,' I tease.

He doesn't say no.

AFTER

'No,' I say, eyeing off the tailor-made black compression suit. It's a full diving suit. Suitable for deep seas. Not mainland living.

'I'm not going out in that. I'm not being seen dead in that at school.'

'I know this is an awkward age to have to be different, but this is an important part of your recovery,' the doctor says. 'Actually, it's the most important thing you can do to help smooth your scar tissue now.'

Another doctor I'll probably never see again. Telling me what to do.

'Will it make my skin perfect?'

'No, Scarlett. Nothing can do that.'

'Then, no. I'm not interested.'

The doctor turns to Dad. Hands him the suit. 'I'll leave this with you. I'd encourage her to wear it.'

'Thanks,' Dad says.

The doctor leaves.

Dad knows better than to tell me to wear it.

'We'll save it in case,' he says. 'Maybe you can start wearing it for a few hours. Just at night and first light.'

FIFTEEN

The first light of our last full day seeps through my curtains. I lie awake, listening to the song of a butcher bird, the laugh of a kookaburra, the distant gargle of the stream.

Tomorrow morning, we will load the car and drive down Matilda Mountain, leaving our crooked cabin in the rear-view mirror. We'll return to our neat white house with its perfect square edges and clipped lawn. And I will go back to school with Pippi, who will tell me exactly what I can and can't do. With Oscar, who doesn't rate me anymore. With Anna, who posts selfies with our friends and their perfectly filtered skin on social media. And I might think I only dreamt that I swam in a cave and fished from a tree and danced on the roof of a mountain hut and met a boy who didn't care what I was like before.

A thick old paperbark, its trunk bent almost in half, reaches out over the waterhole, dipping the ends of its branches into the rippled water like fingers.

'This must be it,' Dad says. 'Dingo Waterhole.'

Two fishing rods jingle over Dad's shoulder and our fold-up

chairs are tucked under his arm, as we stop alongside a wide rippling channel of water. Cicadas screech through the sticky air.

'Lucky we set off early,' he says. 'We're in for a scorcher.'

We set up our chairs by the bank of the waterhole, and Dad teaches me to tie a lure to the end of my rod.

'You want to go nice and easy, okay? Just cast your line out, and slowly reel it back in. We want to see that lure swimming like a fish, not limp like a slug, you got it?'

'Got it.'

My lure is fluoro green and yellow with pins in its body that make it double-jointed so that it will swim through the water like a tiny shiny fish. Dad teaches me to cast, holding a finger on the line as he stretches his rod back, then releasing the line as he throws his lure into the stream.

'Like that! Beautiful cast!'

Beautiful. That word again. Maybe Eamon's right that it's different to pretty. Nobody could call fishing pretty.

Sunshine glitters across the dimpled surface of the waterhole. I watch Dad reel his lure in, the flash of it swimming like an Olympian through the water as he reels it back to the rod.

'Your turn,' he says.

I do as he showed me, reaching my rod back and then thrusting it forward, but I forget to release my finger on the fishing line, so my lure still dangles on the end of my rod.

'Try again.'

I do, and this time I get it, throwing the line and watching as it flies through the air and lands with a plink in the middle of the waterhole.

'That's it! Now reel, reel, reel,' Dad says.

I've just started reeling when the rod jumps in my hand. I almost let go of it.

A tug, and my rod bends nearly in half.

'You've got one! You beauty, you've got one!'

But it feels so heavy, so solid on the end of my line. 'I think it's snagged on the rocks.'

'Oh no, it's not. You've got something, and it's big. Reel it in. Slowly does it.'

I'm standing now, and my line is bending like a candy cane and still I reel. My arms are aching and burning from the effort, but not once does Dad offer to take over for me.

'Keep going, almost there, champ. Here she comes, here she comes . . . '

And suddenly a gaping mouth and a murky head are above the water, followed by a long tubular body in river colours with a smudge of pink along its side. The fish flicks on the end of the line and my arms are shaking now. Just as I think I'm going to drop it on the bank, Dad grabs a net from our bucket and swings it beneath the fish.

'You can let her go,' he says.

I lower it into the net, and Dad unhooks its mouth and pulls the fish out to hold it up.

'That right there is a rainbow trout,' he says. 'Look at the size of her! I'd say she'd be a good couple of kilos. And you reeled that in all by yourself. Incredible!' Dad passes it to me. 'I'll go fill the bucket with water.'

While Dad fills the bucket, I watch my rainbow fish gasping, and I want to put her back. Back into the running water. But this is what it means to live on a mountain, isn't it? This is how Eamon's family survive. By eating what they catch. Not by picking it up from a supermarket shelf, filleted and crumbed beyond all recognition.

Dad comes back with the bucket of water, and as I go to put the fish in, he says, 'Just one photo? Bragging rights?'

My instinct is no. No photos. But then I think of what Eamon said to me last week. *But that outfit's your skin. You're still kinda beautiful.*

It's my skin that's damaged. Only my skin.

'One photo,' I say. 'But I get to delete it if I hate it.'

'Deal.'

I hold the fish in front of me, one hand near its head and one hand at its tummy. I smile as Dad snaps a photo on his phone. Then I put my rainbow fish into the bucket, where it can live a while longer.

'Can I see?'

'She's such a good size,' Dad says, passing me the phone.

Of course, it's not the trout I'm looking at. It's the girl holding it, with the grafted nose and the melted cheek and the arms that look more red than tan, more bone than muscle.

But actually . . . I can stand to look at her. She doesn't make me want to cringe. The girl in the photo doesn't look offensive. Maybe she even looks a tiny bit proud.

Dad reels in the next trout. He's laughing as his rod bends, up on his feet and pulling the fish in from the depths of the waterhole. Sunlight on his ears and in his eyes and through his hair.

I can't remember the last time I saw Dad happy before this trip.

He almost falls into the water, soaking his shoes, and then I'm laughing and he's laughing, and his line goes slack.

'Argh!' But he soon gets another bite. 'These fish are hungry!'

We get bites with almost every cast, reeling in trout after trout, and throwing back the small ones. After only an hour, Dad looks inside the bucket. It's almost full.

'There's enough here to feed a village,' he says.

'Eamon's village.'

'My thoughts exactly. Let's give them a farewell gift, hey?'

'This isn't an excuse to see Claudia one last time, is it?' I tease.

'Geez. Does there have to be an ulterior motive for generosity?'

'No. But I think there is.'

Dad confirms it by smiling to himself.

We drive back to the cabin in the ute, the sun streaming in hot and lazy through the front windscreen. Dreams can't last forever, and our time on the mountain has felt very much like something from a dream. But I guess if dreams can't last forever, nightmares can't either.

As we bump along the gravel track towards the village, kids poke their heads shyly out of caravans to watch us, dirty fingers clinging to doorframes. Dad pulls the handbrake up just shy of Eamon's place.

We get out of the car, Dad carrying the heavy bucket. A hush has fallen over the village and our car doors slam loudly behind us.

Eamon's van door is shut and there's no noise from inside.

'Give it a knock.' Dad nods at the door, but hangs back.

I climb the two steps, aware of all the pairs of small eyes peering at me from behind their own caravan screens.

I knock twice, quietly. No answer.

I turn to Dad and shrug.

Just then, there's a gush of air behind me. A gush of air and Eamon, squinting into the glary day, a couple of dreads sticking up stiffly at the back.

'Oh,' I say. 'Did we . . . wake you?'

He eases the door shut behind him, rubs his eyes. 'Yeah, but that's okay.'

'Sorry.' I step down from the caravan and Eamon follows. 'It was probably time for you to start your day, though. It's nearly lunchtime!'

'Shh, Mum and Cat are still asleep.'

'Sorry, buddy, we didn't know,' Dad says. 'We'll come back later.'

'What's in the bucket?' Eamon takes a step towards Dad and when he peers over the edge, his eyes light up.

'Where'd you get them?'

'Dingo Waterhole.'

'Man,' Eamon says, grinning. 'Just wait till I can drive!'

'These are a gift actually. For you and your mum and the village.'

'Really?' He looks from Dad to me.

'A parting gift. Thanks for sharing your mountain with us, buddy. Now you and the village can have yourselves a little feast.'

Dad hands Eamon the bucket as Claudia emerges barefoot from the caravan. Her long hair is crimped from sleep and her peasant skirt is crushed, but she grabs a bunch of it in her hand as she steps out of the caravan towards us.

'Mum, check it out.' Eamon struggles to lift the waterlogged bucket towards her.

'It's just a small gift,' Dad says, stuffing his hands in his pockets. 'You've been good to Scarlett, good to us both. And we leave tomorrow, so . . .'

Claudia tucks her hair behind her pixie ear. 'That's very generous, thank you.'

Her smile is tired, but a dimple in her cheek struggles through anyway.

'You'll stay for lunch, then? Please, we insist.'

'That's not what I meant.' Dad swallows and looks away. He almost looks nervous. 'We don't expect an invitation. That was just for your hospitality, your kindness.'

Claudia clasps her hands together. 'Well, we can't accept so much if you won't stay and enjoy it with us.'

She nods at Eamon, whose shoulders slump slightly as he extends the bucket back to Dad. But Dad doesn't take the bucket.

'That's an awful lot of fish going to waste then,' Dad says.

'Then let's stay, Dad,' I say.

'Yes, please stay,' Eamon says. 'There's something I want to show Scarlett before you go.'

Dad grins, looks at his feet. 'Looks like I don't have a choice in the matter. My arm's been officially twisted.'

'Good man,' Claudia says. 'Eam, can you go put on some tea?

But be quiet—Cat's still sleeping.' She extends her hand to the wicker chairs and table beside her van. 'Please.'

We all sit down as Eamon disappears into the van and returns with mugs and a teapot. He pours everyone tea and when Claudia sits down beside me, she sighs.

'You okay?' Dad says.

'Oh!' Claudia laughs. 'Did I sigh? Sorry, I'm just a bit tired.'

'Cat doesn't sleep a lot,' Eamon says to us. 'Last night, she barely slept at all, hey, Mum?'

'I'm sorry to hear that,' Dad says. 'Must be very difficult.'

Claudia smiles. 'It has been, but we manage. We always manage, don't we, Eam?'

'Yep. Cat's ours for life.'

And right on cue, Cat emerges. Leaping off the steps of the caravan in one go. She squeals and begins twirling in the sparse grass, hands out either side.

'Well, she's taken a shine to you,' Claudia says to me, smiling. 'She's doing her happy dance. She doesn't do that for just anyone.'

'Really?' I grin, watching her. 'I feel kind of special.'

'Oh, you are,' Claudia says quietly. 'You are.'

By early afternoon, the air is muggy and kids flit in and out of the shady gum trees littered around the camp. I watch Eamon scale and gut the fish.

Before long, fillets of trout are sizzling on the camp stove with garlic and ginger, and they smell amazing. Eamon and I queue up with the rest of the village and load our plates with salad and fish. We find a spare spot on one of the logs around the empty bonfire, which is now just a pile of charred dust. Nobody looks at me strangely, even though it's clear to everyone that I'm an outsider. Dad sits alongside Claudia and whispers something in her ear that makes her laugh.

'It's nice they get along, hey,' Eamon says. 'It's fun having new people around.'

But someone is missing. 'Where's Cat?'

'Over there.' Eamon points to where the stream gurgles past the camp, and there she is, tied up in the leaves of a weeping willow. Clinging to its vines as she sways.

'So is there really a thing you wanted to show me?' I say.

'Absolutely.' Eamon looks at Cat again. 'Actually, we should go while she's distracted. It's not something she can do.'

We scoff the rest of our fish and dump our plates in the communal wash tub. I did catch the fish and he did gut them, so we're not totally lazy.

I think about telling Dad we're heading off, but when I wave my hand at him from the shipping container, he's still talking to Claudia and just waves me off.

Heat is rising from the earth as we walk, baking the ground. The sky has grown fluffy with clouds. We follow the water downstream a while, until we lose all of the village's voices and laughter and it's just us and the cawing of ravens, the cracking of twigs underfoot, lizards scurrying beneath leaves, the babbling of the stream.

Eamon finally stops beneath a wild pear tree. Leaning against its thick twisted trunk is what Eamon has clearly brought me to see.

'You never told me you had a boat.'

'You never asked.' His eyes twinkle, as he strokes the boat like a prized animal. 'Besides, you're the only girl I've ever invited into it.'

He eases it back from the trunk of the tree and pulls the oars out from inside.

'But it's a working boat,' he says. 'Can you row?'

My arms are already weak from this morning's fishing session. But I don't want to be weak. I don't want to be defined by all the things I can't do. Like being pretty and being a dancer and being strong. Today I'm saying no to all of that.

'Give me an oar,' I say. 'I'll learn.'

'Ha!' he says. 'Wildly daring!'

So together we grab the bow of the rowboat and drag it down the embankment into the stream. Eamon holds her steady while I climb in, first one wet foot then the other, the rowboat wobbling with my weight. Then he passes me the oars, pushes the boat from the bank and leaps aboard. The boat rocks violently from his jump and I cling to the sides, laughing.

I hand him an oar and we sit side by side as I learn to put the oar in the water and push back. At first we keep turning because Eamon's strokes are stronger, but we quickly find a happy medium. The water laps against the side of his small boat and we row gently downstream with the current.

'Something I didn't tell you about the thing that tried to kill me,' I say.

'Yeah?'

'It took most of the muscle from my arms. I was told I'd never get full use of them again.'

He raises his eyebrows. 'Aren't doctors ridiculous? Think they know everything!'

'No, actually, they would've been right. But Dad wasn't as quick to give up on me as they were. Dad is the kind who just doesn't quit.'

'Well, you can do pretty much everything. I'd never have known. You're pretty amazing, you know.'

I feel the blood pump to my cheek. *Amazing*. The word makes me shy. Besides Dad, nobody has made me feel amazing since the accident, except maybe this boy now, rowing alongside me.

And maybe I'm just making excuses for why I can't dance. Because the truth is a shiver of fear crawls up my spine at the thought of being back on a stage, dancing for a crowd.

Eamon puts his hand on mine and raises my scarred arm into the sky.

'This girl's walked through fire!'

I laugh, and he lets my arm go so we can keep our rhythm rowing.

'Fish Boy and Fire Girl, huh?'

He smiles. 'What a combination!'

'And Cat can be the mermaid. Would she jump in if you took her rowing?'

'Definitely. Without one single doubt. And she'd take off downstream faster than I could catch her!'

'How far does the creek go?'

'All the way to the catchment, if you could get down the waterfall.'

'Yeah, let's not try that,' I say, laughing.

We row and chat as the sky grows dull and dark, and the mosquitoes start to whine. I try not to think of all that waits for me when I get back home. Of boys like Oscar and Byron. Eamon has changed the way I'll look at them, with his easy company. He's very different to the boys I've known. I don't need to dress in the best clothes, or put on make-up, or fear being ranked on some horrible scale. Eamon is brave enough to be real, so I feel safe being real back.

A fat drop of water hits my arm, and I wipe it away. Another soon follows.

'It's raining,' I say, holding my hands palm up to feel it. 'We're rowing in the rain!'

But Eamon has stopped rowing. He's looking behind us.

'Whoa,' he breathes.

I look over my shoulder, then I stop rowing too.

Behind us, a thick black ribbon of cloud twists across the sky.

'Let's turn around,' he says.

Eamon spins us so that we're now facing the large mass of cloud, but rowing away from it.

'I've never seen anything like it,' Eamon says, looking up at the dark funnelling mass of cloud slowly suffocating the landscape. 'It's moving pretty quick.'

I watch the blackened clouds swell across the sky.

We row hard, but my arms are burning from the strain of going against the water, and we're going slowly. Too slowly.

Fat drops of rain hit the water, kicking up spray. They hit the boat with a plinking noise. They hit our skin with small thwacks.

The dark cloud is circular now, stacked like plates in the sky, swirling clockwise as it spreads across the sky.

'Give me your oar,' Eamon says.

I don't argue, just hand it over and move out of his way.

Mosquitoes whine in our ears as the sky grows an eerie shade of midnight.

A fork of lightning shatters the dark. Thunder rattles the bones of the boat.

'It's gonna hit any second. We have to get out. Now.'

Eamon rows frantically to the bank.

'Get out,' he says again.

I leap out one side into the water and he leaps out the other, as leaves begin spiralling madly through the sky.

'Grab it and pull,' he says, tugging at the boat.

I grab it, but the bank here is rocky and steep.

'That's got hail in it. We need cover,' he says.

I heave at the boat with all my strength, really pull it. Up it comes, inch by inch.

'Pull harder!' Eamon says.

He doesn't make allowances for my weak arms. *No excuses*, Dad says in my ear. *One punch at a time.* One pull at a time.

We wrench the boat up as a wall of wind slams into us, flipping the boat onto its back. Wild and untamed, the wind howls through the trees and makes their limbs tremble like toothpicks.

A second fork of lightning splits the sky with explosive force. It looks like something from the end of the world. Like nothing I've seen before. Like a giant hand has picked up our mountain and is shaking it loose.

The heavens open and rain pours down around us. Big hard drops smashing against the trees and turning the landscape white. Something large hits the ground in front of us and bounces into the air like a tennis ball.

'Hail! Quick, flip the boat!'

We flip the boat beneath the shelter of a gum tree, and huddle under it before sealing it over us like a cupped hand. Rain thrashes down hard against the tin, hemming us in, and water pours up from the ground, like it's the earth that's crying and not the sky. Branches clatter, lashed by wind and hail, and a crack hits the side of the boat.

The storm is too loud even to talk, so we just crouch together and I shiver, even though I'm not cold. Eamon grabs hold of my hand. I squeeze, and he squeezes back.

Hail bangs against the underside of the boat, leaving dents the size of fists, and smashing the branches above us. Rivers of water run past, soaking us through until we're both sopping. Eamon is shaking too, as the ground beneath us trembles.

We stay like this a long time. Until the hail stops denting the boat, until the clatter of the branches quiets and debris stops scraping past. We stay huddled together until all we can hear is the heavy drumming of rain.

'I think we should go,' Eamon says in my ear.

'No.'

'Your dad will be worried.'

I hadn't thought about that. Dad's safety or Dad's worrying. What if he came out into the storm to try and find me? What if he's lying somewhere, pummelled by hail the size of tennis balls?

'Let's go,' I say.

So we lift the boat and crawl on hands and knees out from under it.

The world is changed. Splintered. Snapped. Trees have been torn limb from limb, another tree uprooted from the earth, branches tossed like straw across the ground. A wet carpet of leaves and twigs. The wind has passed, but not the rain. It pours in sheets from the sky like it has no beginning and no end. Rivers run along the ground and waterfall over the bank, into the stream.

Eamon takes my hand and pulls me. Uphill we run, doubled over, squinting against the rain, soggy wet, with water squelching up through our shoes and down through our clothes and running cold dribbles along our spines.

We stagger and we fall and we run, until the village is in sight and I am breathless. Until I think I can't go another step, but still Eamon pulls me.

'Come on,' he urges. 'You've survived worse than this.'

I fall.

'Come on, Scarlett.'

His words gnaw at my back. So I pull myself up. I push myself on.

We stumble into the camp, and then spotlights are shining on us and people are running through the rain and arms are pulling us in. In where it's dry. Inside the hall full of warm bodies. Full of voices and laughter and sheer relief. Full of my dad, who is crying and pulling me close and squeezing the life out of me.

'Let's get you dry,' Dad says. 'You're frozen to the bone.'

And my teeth are chattering too hard to answer. But the answer is yes. Yes, please.

I look for Eamon, expecting him to be wrapped in Claudia's arms. But Claudia isn't hugging him. She isn't saying, 'Let's get you dry.' She isn't laughing or crying with relief. She's ghostly pale. And she's looking past Eamon.

'Where's Cat?' Her voice is quiet.

It stills the hall.

'Cat?'

'She was with you, wasn't she?'

Even in the dark, I can see Eamon's skin shed its colour.

'Eamon, where is she?'

AFTER

'Where is she? Where's the patient?' the doctor says lightly.

I'm balancing cereal on the end of a long-handled spoon and lifting it to my mouth. A few grains fall off, but I catch the others in my mouth.

'Well done,' the doctor says, smiling at me. 'That's an improvement from a week ago.'

With a special spoon, I can now feed myself soft things. Yoghurt, cereal, custard, rice.

It feels pathetic and like I've climbed a mountain at the same time.

But then the doctor turns to Dad.

'She's making great progress,' he says. 'She'll likely never have full use of her arms again, but these are great first steps.'

I drop the spoon. It hits the edge of the tray, splashing milk and cereal as it clatters to the floor.

'I'll get you a new spoon,' the doctor says, buzzing the nurse.

Then, 'She's lost a significant amount of muscle tissue, so we have to be realistic about her recovery.' He says it as though I'm not right here. Listening. 'She's lucky to have kept all her digits. Most full-thickness burns to the limbs result in amputations. I'll organise the occupational therapist to talk to you about having your home modified accordingly.'

When the doctor leaves, I say to Dad, 'I don't want to change our house.'

'I know.'

'He said I won't be able to use my arms properly again.'

'Well, that just gives us something to prove, doesn't it?' Dad doesn't look me in the eye, though. 'There's nothing half as determined as an underdog.'

'What's an underdog?' I ask.

'Someone nobody expects anything from. A person with nothing to lose. They're the most dangerous kind of opponent. Mark Twain once said, "It's not the size of the dog in the fight, it's the size of the fight in the dog." You ever heard that before?'

I shake my head.

'Well, you might be small, champ, but you're a little fighter. And your dad's a big fighter. And we're gonna show them who you are.'

SIXTEEN

'Show me where she is.' Claudia's voice is a whisper.

Eamon wipes a shaky hand over his mouth as he stares out the open door at the tormented landscape. 'I don't know.'

'She's out there,' Claudia says. 'Isn't she?'

Eamon looks blankly at the driving rain as Claudia slips on her sandals and walks out into it.

'Cat!' she calls. But the wind swallows her voice. 'Cat!'

Dad goes after her, squinting into the rain as he talks to her, but Claudia doesn't seem to notice him. She keeps calling, but her voice is drowned by the drumming of the rain on the steel roof. She turns a slow revolution, a desperate dance, as she peers through the rain, her dress clinging to her thin body like wet tissue.

Dad guides her back inside. Claudia's limp dress hangs off her hips like they're a coat hanger. Her face has a sickly yellow tinge, hands gripping Dad's so hard her knuckles are white. Opa is beside her now, and Claudia lets go of Dad's hands and falls against Opa's shoulder.

Silent tears mingle with rain water, running little rivers down her face.

'The creeks are rising,' she says. 'I can hear them gushing.'

Claudia, who knows life isn't perfect. Claudia, who belongs to Cat. Cat, who loves the water. Eamon's words return to me. *Once you get her in the water, good luck getting her out.* I look over at Eamon. He is made of stone. Staring. Staring out into the wild landscape. His silence scares me.

'She's out there,' Claudia gasps, pulling away from Opa. 'My baby girl is out there.' She heads for the door again, but Opa holds her.

'Wait!' Dad says. 'Claudia, we need you. Let's think this through.'

She turns around.

'How long do we think she's been gone?' Dad asks.

Nobody answers. But my last memory is clear. 'When we left, she was playing by the willow tree. That was around two o'clock, I think. Maybe three.'

'She sat next to me to eat,' says little Heidi in her still-scruffy pigtails. 'Then she ran off with Chief. I told her not to, but she didn't listen.'

Chief. I hadn't noticed him missing.

'So she might have the dog with her?' Dad says.

Claudia rushes over to Heidi, kneels down so that she's level with her and grabs her by the shoulders so that Heidi is looking her in the eyes.

'Did you see where she ran, Heidi? What direction, sweetie?'

Heidi shrugs. 'I didn't see.'

Dad crouches down next to Claudia, so they're both level with her.

'We need you to think really hard about this, okay, little matey? It's really important.'

Heidi bites her lip. 'I think the track. The one to the cabin.'

'The cabin,' Dad says. 'My ute. Let's go.'

Claudia runs out into the rain and Dad follows. I hear the faint roar of an engine and watch through the open doorway as his ute wheels spin in the slick mud before tracking away, twin beams piercing through the gloom.

Eamon is very still. He hasn't moved or spoken. Even his freckles have paled under the dim generator light.

'You okay?' I say.

He doesn't respond. But when I follow his line of sight, I see he's listening to his opa, who has gathered a few of the adults around him.

'The flood waters are rising. There'll be a flash flood through by morning. Creeks will burst their banks. I need you all to understand there's a very real chance that if we don't find our little girl tonight, we're not going to find her at all. Everyone grab a torch. We'll head downstream. We want our little girl home tonight. However that happens, we're getting her home.'

However that happens? An ominous vision flashes through my mind. Opa carrying a long limp girl in his arms, dark braids dripping from her loose neck.

I shake it.

Cat. She's written in everyone's thoughts.

Eamon starts visibly trembling beside me. A full-body tremble.

'It's my job,' he says quietly. 'Cat. It's my job to look after her. She's terrified of storms. She'll be calling for me.'

'Eamon, stop,' I say. I'm surprised by the fierceness of my words. But this is not the first crisis I've experienced. 'You can't afford to think like that. Now's the time to act. Think later.'

A hand rests on Eamon's shoulder and I look up to see Opa draping a large jacket across Eamon's small shoulders.

'You kids need to get dry and stay put. Look after the little ones. We'll find her.'

But Eamon dumps the jacket on the floor and makes a break for the open door.

Opa steps in front of him, blocking his path.

'Don't be silly, son.'

'Let me go.' Eamon's voice breaks as he tries to push past Opa. 'I'll find her. It's my job. Cat's my—' But he can't even say the word. He is sobbing and pushing, trying to get past Opa, but the old man is too strong.

'This is no time to be a hero, son. What you need to be right now is a kid.' He pushes Eamon back inside. 'You want to do your job as her brother?'

Eamon looks up at Opa, his eyes brimming with tears.

'Best thing you can do for Cat is stay calm and let us look for her. Last thing we need is to be off in the night chasing more lost kids.'

But Eamon won't be dismissed. Not that easily. He still struggles against his opa, gasping, his face wracked with the kind of pain I felt when they ripped off my dressings.

'Think of your mother.' Opa's voice is firm and quiet.

'She doesn't deserve to lose two kids.'

That stops Eamon thrashing. Makes his arms drop weakly by his sides.

The sky lights up with jagged forks and thunder booms overhead as the small group gather torches. Eamon steps aside until he's back against the corrugated walls of the hall. Then he slides down into a crouch, his head between his hands.

'Focus on the water,' Opa says as they head out into the night. 'Look for something pink. Bright pink she's wearing. That girl loves water.'

Opa's words are the trigger.

I have seen Cat in the water, frolicking in the caves. A place made for mermaids. Protected from hail and wind and rain. But not from floods.

'I know where she is,' I say.

Eamon looks up, locks eyes with me. And in that moment, I see that he knows too.

We start at Eamon's caravan, where he rummages under his bed for a torch.

He throws me a jumper of Cat's and a pair of her tights to change into. He grabs a pair of track pants, a shirt and a jacket for himself.

We change quickly and start out on foot for the cabin. The wind moans like a restless spirit through the trees and there are no stars to guide us. Just muddy earth caking to our shoes like clay, making them heavy and slippery.

But nothing can stop us. Not the cold wind that bites at our wet faces, or the rain that runs new rivers down our dry shirts.

We have one focus. One destination. We don't even talk.

We pass the cabin, but Dad's ute isn't there. Lights in the distance tell us they're still searching. But they won't find her. Cat is a mermaid, and mermaids don't live on land.

We reach the creek where I first danced, and I barely recognise it. Swollen and foamy, muddy and roaring. Water gushes under and around the ivy-covered log, sticks and grass banking up on the upstream side.

Eamon lights the way and I cross first, him right behind me. The wet moss on the log is slippery, and the soles of my shoes are still caked with mud. This is no time for pirouettes. One of my feet slips off the log, and Eamon catches my arm. I don't look at the roaring water below. I can't afford to think about falling. Eamon and I wobble together as I steady myself, still not a word spoken. Then we continue across the log. I jump down on the far side of the bank, sliding in a slick of mud. But I get up and we keep moving, like we're one person instead of two. One focus. One mission.

The path to the cave is slippery with wet leaves, and I take another slide down a rocky embankment. Eamon helps me up again, and we keep going.

Suddenly he stops. 'You hear that?'

I listen. Above the rain and the wind, a noise. Repetitive, echoing, deep.

Somewhere, a dog is barking.

'Chief!' Eamon starts running, knocking small branches and twigs out of his path, torchlight bouncing across the shiny earth.

Eamon takes a tumble, hits his knee. Yells. But he's up again. Neither of us able to slow down. Any fall worth it, just to get there. So we run, crashing through the bush as the barking gets louder, panting as the mouth of the forbidden caves comes in sight, and with it a mountain lion of a dog. Glowing white beneath the torchlight. He barks as we approach.

'C'mere, boy,' Eamon says, and Chief's ears drop back.

Then he's leaping towards us, and us towards him. He pelts into Eamon, knocking him over, his entire body wagging with his tail, his tongue licking Eamon's face.

But we're not here for a reunion with Chief.

Eamon pushes Chief off and gets up.

'Where is she? Where is she, boy?'

We shine the torch into the cave and the light bounces off its glistening walls. The cave is dark and menacing in the night, all the magic gone.

We step in anyway. Chief barks, but won't follow. The noise inside is thundering. A persistent roar like a monster heaving. A dripping, rushing place of terror.

The roof is littered with green pinpricks of light, like stars. A warped fairyland. Except this is too dark, too dangerous to be fairyland. And the stalactites hang from the ceiling like rows of shark teeth.

The gushing water drowns out our footsteps. Water that covers the ledges, covers our ankles as it rushes past. The caves are quickly filling from all the rain washing down the mountain.

'Cat!' Eamon calls. His voice rebounds back at us.

The ledge around the cave is slippery and uneven, and we can't see where we're walking or where it ends. We cling to the wall of the cave and inch our way deeper into its belly. Eamon flicks the beam of light through the murky water. No longer jade-coloured, but muddy and foamy, like the creeks.

'Cat!'

A chill runs the length of my spine. I haven't thought about what we might find. Or how we might manage that.

But then, a shriek.

A laugh.

A gleeful sound in the horrifying darkness.

'Cat!'

Eamon is running now, water sloshing around his ankles. Shining his light into the soupy foam, the beam passes over twigs and branches.

'There!' I say suddenly. 'Pink! Over there!'

It was just a glimpse. One bright flash in the water, one shard of hope. But Eamon sweeps the light back and finds it. Finds her.

Another shriek.

Cat, her pink shirt on, washing around in the flood waters.

I almost leap in after her, but I don't have to. Because Eamon shoves the torch into my hand, strips off his jacket and jumps in. Shoes, pants and all.

Cat is being swept against the sides of the rock wall in the water, like a wispy dress in a washing machine. She doesn't seem to care, or even feel the pain of the gritty limestone grazing her skin.

She shrieks at the sight of Eamon and tries to swim away, but the water washes her back against the cave wall again. Water is everywhere, pouring like a waterfall into the pool, filling it higher til it's no longer a pool, just a cave full of water. Water that's rising. It's halfway up my calves now.

'Cat, we need to go,' Eamon says.

She squeals and turns on her back, looking up at the glow-worms that light the ceiling. But Eamon reaches her and pulls her to him in a hug.

'You're a rogue,' he says. 'You know how worried we've all been?'

He takes her by the hand, and even though she dead-weights herself on her back and the water is washing them towards the wall, Eamon battles her to the edge of the cave, to the torchlight. But just as he reaches the ledge, a wall of water washes into the pool and Eamon disappears. The water knocks me against the side of the cave, the roar of it terrifying.

But I can see Cat, so I reach out for her hand and haul her up, dripping wet, purple-lipped and shaking.

Eamon surfaces in the swirling torrent, struggles against the current until he reaches the ledge again and pulls himself out. He's panting and shivering, but in the flash of torchlight, I see that his eyes are shining.

He wraps Cat up in his arms and holds her close.

'Don't you ever do that to me again,' he says into her hair. 'Don't you ever.'

Another wave of water rushes into the pool.

'Let's go,' I say.

We stumble back towards the mouth of the cave. Water is now spewing out of it and sliding down the mountain. The rain is lighter now, more a shush of white than a torrent. Chief is patiently waiting for us, and he leaps at Cat when he sees her, licking furiously at her hands.

I hand Eamon his sodden jacket and he throws it around Cat, keeping hold of her hand. Cat is cold and thin beneath the torchlight. We need to get her warm, and back to Claudia.

Claudia, who must be sick with fear.

We half stumble, half run back to the river. We find the log that will guide us home, but then I look at Chief. Chief, who is backing away from the roaring creek. Who fell off last time when the log was dry.

'You go first,' Eamon says to me. 'See if Chief follows.'

Water is pouring beneath the log and bursting around it. One wrong step, one slip, and I'll be carried away by it.

I close my eyes to block it out. Balance is something a dancer must master and I have always had good balance. I take a deep breath. Pretend I'm dancing on stage. Wiping the leaves and mud from my shoes, I put one foot on the log, then the other, and go, arms out either side. I don't think about it, I just move. One foot in front of the other, until I'm across the other side, leaping down to the bank.

I turn around, but Chief hasn't followed me across the log.

'Come on, Chief!' I pat my hands against my legs. 'C'mon, boy!'

I'm not sure he'll make it across, but what other choice is there? The river's rapidly rising. Soon he'll have no chance.

'Chief, go!' Eamon says.

Chief scrabbles at the slippery log, but falls back. Puts one paw tentatively in the rushing water, then pulls it out again.

He's smart enough to know not to leap right in. He'd rather stay with his people.

'Maybe when you come across?' I say.

'Okay, Cat, let's go.' Eamon nudges her ahead of him.

Cat doesn't think about it. As if she crosses the log in these conditions every day, she steps up and just starts walking, Eamon behind her. But then her foot slips on the wet moss, and she wobbles. I hold my breath. Eamon steadies her from behind, just like he did with me. Somehow, she regains her balance.

'Careful,' I yell. 'Slow and steady!'

They make it to the end of the log, and Cat jumps down at the exact same moment that Eamon slips.

I see it happen in slow motion, his foot sliding off the log, him overbalancing.

He seems to fall into the water gracefully. In snapshots.

I drop the torch equally slowly. It blinks out. I reach for him in slow motion.

Time stops for a second.

Then Eamon hits the rushing water with his knee, which buckles and gets sucked out from beneath him by the current. My hand is reaching for his, his hand reaching back for mine.

Our eyes catch, and there is a look in his that I'll never forget. The look of fear. The same look I must have had in Gran's car on the Mitchell Motorway. *This is how I'll die*.

Our reaching hands meet and we grab hold, but the current

is strong and sucking and my arms have never felt weaker. I grip his wrist like a monkey and he grips mine in turn. I can feel him pulling, wanting me to pull him out with equal force, but it's a force I don't have. All I can do is hold onto him with my weak muscles in my damaged arms.

So I hold on, as strong as I can, stronger than I ever thought I possibly could, stronger than any boxing session I've ever had with Dad. But the water won't stop. It's stronger than both of us. It moves with a powerful, tireless energy. And it drags Eamon under with it.

Chief begins barking. A deep, urgent noise. He won't stop. And suddenly he is charging through the water, leaping towards us, towards Eamon. But the water is too deep and too fast and he loses momentum. Chief is washed downstream, until I can't hear any more barking.

Chief! My mind is screaming. But I know all I can afford to spend my energy on. And it's not Chief. It is only this. Holding on. Second by second. To this boy. Who I don't want to die.

The water is gushing over Eamon's face now and all I can see in the dark is a mop of his hair swishing above the waterline like knotted seaweed.

Then his grip on my wrist goes limp.

'No,' I say, gritting my teeth and holding on tighter.

But Eamon's not holding onto me anymore. It's only me. My strength so weak in my pathetic arms. But that weak strength is the only thing keeping Eamon from being sucked away forever.

I see the people at the scene of the car fire. Smashing in the windows for me.

Tugging, hands gripping. Pulling.

Hear Dad in our training sessions.

Harder, champ. You can go harder than that.

Remember Eamon running with me through the storm. Taking my hand.

Come on. You've survived worse than this.

So even though he can't hear me, I find myself yelling at Eamon.

'Stay with me!' I roar. 'I'll get you out!'

Cat starts squealing, screeching. I don't know if she understands.

'I've got him,' I say. Except I'm crying, and I have no strength left to pull. Or even speak. The last strength I have is channelled into fingers that refuse to let go.

If I can't hold on anymore, if I have to let him go, I could go with him. Let us be dragged down into the depths of the water and end it all.

That's what I've wished for, isn't it? To have died back there on the Mitchell Motorway in that burning car? To have died a beautiful girl, instead of being left living as an ugly one? Well, now's my chance. I could do it. Nobody would know I let myself go. Cat keeps everyone's secrets. And it would be just a sad tale of two kids who drowned in a storm.

But I can't do it to Eamon. It's Eamon keeping my fingers burning in their grip. Eamon, who needs to look after Cat. Eamon, who loves Cat more than anyone. Eamon, who Claudia needs too. It might be okay for the river to sweep me away, swallow me whole, but it's not okay for Eamon.

Maybe it's not even okay for me. Because despite all the pain and all the scars, somewhere deep in my gut there is a hard, shiny thing. A strength to keep going. And it's only small, but it will grow the more I flex it, like the muscles in my arms. And I may not have my pretty skin and my lovely face and my strong arms anymore. But I have *this*. And it will last longer than prettiness. It will grow all the days of my life, if I let it.

I didn't get to decide about the fire, but I get to decide this. I get to choose for Eamon and for me. And for Dad, who I can't leave. And for Claudia, who I can't hurt. And for Cat, who I can't deprive.

My ending isn't here, it isn't now. Neither is Eamon's.

A bark breaks through the rushing water. I am hallucinating. But then it happens again, right at my ear. And there is Chief, barking by the edge of the creek at Eamon. Urging him out of the water. Like he knows this is wrong. So very wrong.

Chief gives me the final push I need. I reach in and grasp hold of that hard, shiny thing inside me. And this is how I give one last, inhuman reef of my arms, with strength I didn't know I could find. And this is how I pull Eamon out of that thundering foamy water, where he flops lifeless onto the bank.

I can't move. I can't help him anymore. Every last drop of every last thing I had was spent getting him out.

Why is Chief still barking? Why is Cat still screaming?

Why is Eamon still not moving?

I crawl to him, where he lies with his face in the mud. And I grab hold of his sopping dreadlocks, turning his freckled face towards me.

His skin is as white as the moon and water dribbles from his purple lips. No smile greets me, just the whites of his eyes. The water has drowned out his spirit and left us with just a body.

I am crying, and feebly shaking his shoulders. I am yelling now, in a language I can't even understand because I have lost my own. I am slumped over his body, and my tears are hitting his face, but not waking him.

Then his body is lit up. And for one awful second, I think they're taking him. Angels, come to raise him up and take his body.

But then Dad is crouching beside me. Not talking to me, just turning Eamon over, shoving his fingers down his throat. And water is gushing, gushing out of him like the water in the river gushing over the log.

Dad flips Eamon onto his back and starts compressions on his chest. I yell at him.

But Dad ignores me, pushing down on his chest over and over. I hear something crack.

I turn around and Claudia is on her knees in the waterlogged mud, her hands pressed to her mouth. She doesn't seem to care that her floral dress is soaked in mud up to her thighs. I want to tell her to get up. To stop looking like that.

I saved him. I pulled him out. He's okay.

But a howl comes from her mouth. Or her throat. Or somewhere deep inside her chest. And it doesn't sound like the voice of a woman. Not that clear pretty voice she sang with only nights ago on the guitar. It sounds like the cry of an animal. A wounded, tortured animal.

I cover my ears, but not my eyes.

She raises her face to the rain, and its wetness cloaks her.

'Please!' she cries. 'Please!'

Cat rocks on the ground next to her, moaning and biting at her hand.

I lie next to Eamon in the soggy mud.

Numb. Watching.

Feeling nothing.

Not fear. Not pain. Not heartache.

Cold, white nothing.

Because Eamon will be okay.

He has to be.

He is a fish, born into water.

And fish don't drown.

AFTER

I am drowning.

The sun bursts over the sea as it rises and Dad coaxes me out further.

My arms are stiff and unfamiliar. My brain remembers how to lift them, how to swim the strokes, but my arms don't.

They can't move that way anymore.

A wave lifts me, carrying me away from Dad.

I am a seal in my compression suit.

I kick my legs. They still work, but I want to cry as the wave sucks me in and spits me out on the shore.

Instead, I sit on the sand in the sucking waves and let myself get pulled back and forth.

I got my bronze lifesaving medallion last year.

I had to swim laps of the fifty metre pool, fully clothed, all the strokes perfect.

I had to tread water wearing shoes.

Tow someone along behind me.

Now I can't swim a single stroke.

Can't lift my arms above my head.

Can't catch a wave.

'Try again,' Dad calls from behind the breakers.

I pick myself up. Go back out. Same result.

Dumped. Slammed on the sand. Grit in my teeth and my ears and plastered through my hair.

But Dad doesn't let me off easy.

He never does.

He swims into shore. Picks up the hand mitts. His favourite form of torture.

'Five of your best,' he says. 'Start with the left.'

I try to make a fist. My fingers curl over. It's as close as I get.

Dad slides on the boxing mitts, holds them down at my stomach.

'High as you can,' he says.

I clench my teeth. Will my arm to move.

It's not a punch. Just a light tap on the mitt. He even has to bring the mitt towards me so that I can reach it.

'Good. Again. Now the other one. Again.'

We go until I'm aching all over.

'There are two things in life you can depend on,' Dad says. 'What are they?'

He says this to me every morning.

'Choices and consequences,' I say.

'And what do you choose?'

'Not to give up.'

'That's my girl.'

So I keep pushing until I want to cry.

Until I tell Dad to leave me alone.

Until people start seeping down for their morning jogs along the beach.

Looking at the man training the girl in the compression suit.

That's when it's time to go home and Dad bundles me up.

SEVENTEEN

Dad bundles me up in a scratchy old blanket to keep me warm.

'You're in shock,' he says.

Eamon is gone. Claudia is gone. The storm is gone.

The night is not gone. It comes back to me in snapshots.

Dad pumping Eamon's chest. Eamon coughing, vomiting.

'He's breathing.'

Claudia dialling out on Dad's phone.

The ute fishtailing in the mud on its way to meet the ambulance.

Dad driving us back to the village.

Chief jumping down from the back of the ute, washed black with mud.

Light bursting out from the hall. Beams painting Dad and Cat.

Opa running forward, scooping her into his arms.

The shake of Dad's shoulders, head bent into his fingers.

Hands on Dad. Many hands, strong hands. Hands of thanks, hands of praise, hands of comfort.

Dad driving us back to the cabin in silence.

Time has passed, but my understanding of time is lost.

The night dense and sludgy, water slicked across a rainbow windscreen.

My eyes are thick. My head is swirling. One word runs through it.

Eamon.

Eamon wiping grubby hands down his pants. His scratchy voice. His shiny eyes when we found Cat. In the mountain water. Water meant to heal people, not kill them.

I want to hear Eamon laugh at Chief's big tongue on my face. I want to hear him say, 'Get down! Down, boy!' I want him to tell me that Cat is his favourite, that he loves her the most. I won't even get jealous this time. I saved him for Cat. He just needs to come back for Cat.

Please let him be okay.

We stop out the front of the cabin. Its tin roof overhung with twigs, leafy branches, debris.

The power is out. Like we knew it would be. But the water is on.

So Dad runs me a shower. He runs it until the bathroom is a fog of steam.

Then he puts me in the bathroom. Shuts the door behind me.

I don't undress, though. I sink down on the floor.

Nothing. I feel nothing.

A knock. 'You under yet?'

Numb fingers peel off clothes.

I shower under stinging needles of spray. Hot jets. Painful heat.

But I feel only ice. Ice from the inside, numbing the outside.

I notice my legs shaking, but I can't feel them beneath me.

My hands are red and swollen and scratched. Foreign hands to match my foreign body. I don't own them.

I stare straight ahead at the cracked tiles of the shower wall.

I don't know how long I stand there. One minute or one hour. I stand under the water until my insides feel like liquid instead of ice. I don't reach for the bar of soap or the toothbrush. I just stand still under the spray until Dad knocks on the door again.

'I think that's enough, champ.'

I instruct myself like I do at home.

Get out of the shower, Scarlett. One step, two steps, that's it. Grab a towel. Wrap it around you. Pat yourself dry. That's good.

The fog in the bathroom slowly clears and I see the misty shape of a girl in the mirror. I can't see her face. It wouldn't matter if I could.

I pull on warm pyjamas. Then I let Dad guide me to bed. Steering me by shoulders that feel a hundred years old. He peels back the blankets, and I fall into the sheets.

I don't remember closing my eyes.

When I open my eyes again, it's first light.

Something is wrong. Badly wrong. I know it in my gut. I just can't quite place it.

Then I remember Eamon.

And I remember something else, from the deeper reaches of my mind.

There's something I need to do.

I slip out of bed. My arms are stiff and sore as I dress, but I grit my teeth and push through the pain. I wince with every step I take away from the cabin, as I drag myself up the muddy track. My arms tremble, my shoulders burn and earth slips beneath my boots. The land has been decimated, trees blown sideways, uprooted, snapped. But I grab hold of the broken branches, biting my lip with the pain, as I pull myself, arm by arm and step by step, up the steep incline.

I want this more than I have wanted anything. And maybe, if I make my wish to the universe from the highest peak of our mountain, it will be heard. From the magical spot at the top of the world, where little girls can fly free and boys can surely be mended.

Rain begins to drift like soft feathers from the sky. It kisses my skin.

When I reach the top of the mountain, I don't stop.

I haul myself onto the roof of Tilly's Hut. Onto that ridgeline I danced along so long ago. Then I stand tall, balancing my arms out either side. I close my eyes and send up my wish.

My wish for one boy.

Who is also a fish.

That he will walk again. And swim again. And laugh again.

That he will be healed.

I send the wish one hundred times. I'll never know if Tilly's bird-girl flew off the cliff or leapt to her death. Maybe Claudia was right and Tilly didn't want us to know. Maybe we're meant to decide for ourselves. But today, I choose that the bird-girl flew.

I stretch out my arms slowly and begin to dance beneath the cloudy mottled sky. Along the ridgeline, I am the bird-girl.

Leaping, hoping, falling, flying.

I am dancing for you, Eamon. I am dancing now, can't you see?

'Can't you see we all get to tell our own stories?' Nikki spins her chair to face me. 'When I was a baby, my mother gave me up for adoption. That's how my story started. But that's not my whole story. We all have good and bad things happen to us and they balance each other, like night and day.'

'But some people get more bad stuff than others,' I say. 'What happens when people get too broken?'

Nikki thinks for a minute. 'Have you ever looked through a kaleidoscope? What have you seen?'

'Colours, shapes.'

She smiles. 'Broken fragments still make a beautiful rainbow. Now, I have a job for you, Scarlett. I want you to tell me your story.'

'My story?'

'Yes. And you can focus on the fire, if you like, or the scars, or the medical procedures. But is that your whole story? Are you only *what happened to you in the fire? You're free to tell your story however you like, but the way you tell it is important, especially the way you tell it to yourself. You're the narrator. The main character. And you can let other*

people, like Pippi, tell your story, if you want, and they can decide what you can and can't do. Or, you can take the pen. And even though you can't rewrite the past, you can decide what happens next. So tell me, how does Scarlett's story end?'

EIGHTEEN

It's the end. We pack our bags quietly as we farewell our mountain home. I watch Dad slide the boxing mitts into his suitcase and zip it shut.

Dad, throwing in the towel for me.

I unzip his bag. Pull out the mitts. Hand them to him.

'Show me what you've got. No excuses,' I say.

Dad puts the mitts back in his suitcase.

'Not today, champ.'

He zips it shut.

'It's going to be okay,' I say firmly. 'Don't you dare be giving up.'

'Never,' Dad says, but his voice is hollow. 'I'll never give up on you.'

But he won't look me in the eye, and suddenly I want to know if he's heard an update on Eamon. I want to know, but . . . I also don't want to know.

The doctors are calling it a non-fatal drowning. Non-fatal doesn't mean Eamon will be okay. It just means he won't die. Eamon doesn't belong in the city, or in a hospital. Fish belong in the country, in the water. They belong in the wild.

I focus on the Eamon of yesterday afternoon. The one pushing the boat out into the water, leaping aboard, teaching me to row. But his other face seeps into my thoughts. The white face with purple lips dribbling water.

Dad is loading up the back of the ute when his phone rings. He looks at it.

'Private number,' he says. Looks at me.

He turns his back. But I already know who it is.

'Put it on loudspeaker.'

Dad ignores me.

'Claudia,' he says, and his voice cracks. 'How is he?'

He listens for a moment, then hangs his head.

My blood chills.

But then he hits loudspeaker, and I see that he's smiling. Nodding at me, tears in his eyes.

'He's going to be in for a few days,' Claudia says over the speaker. 'His oxygen levels need to come up and he's still got a bit of fluid in his lungs, but they said he's one of the lucky ones. He's going to make a complete recovery.'

I tip my head back to the sky, close my eyes and let the tears slide down my face.

The universe. It heard me.

When we pull into the driveway, I can smell Gran's chicken soup wafting through the windows. She's cooked my favourite for dinner.

And before we're even out of the car, she is at my door, wrenching it open, holding me close, clutching at my hair.

'My girl,' she whispers. 'My precious, precious girl.'

Gran doesn't call me pretty anymore, but I'll take precious. Precious things are for holding onto. And she does hold onto me. For a very long time, she holds me. Until I think she's never going to let me go. But eventually she does let go, and when she does I see that her face is slicked wet.

'I'm sorry,' she whispers, her eyes haunted as they search mine. 'Sorry for slamming on the brakes. Sorry for not being able to save you from that fire. I'm so very sorry, sweetie, for everything you've lost.' And Gran's eyes are spilling with fresh tears that run in wobbly, unfamiliar patterns down her face. 'I thought we'd lost you last night. I thought I'd never again get the chance to tell you what a beautiful girl you are, Scarlett. Strong and brave and graceful.' She smiles through watery eyes at me. 'You still have beauty in spades.'

I pull Gran tight and feel the bones in her rib cage beneath my fingers.

Gran is the woman who took me on as her own, who loved me and raised me without complaining that it wasn't her job. She's not perfect, she says wacky things sometimes, but I'm not looking for perfect. I'm just looking for the people who are mine. The ones who love me.

And I don't want to hold onto my anger. Anger is a kind of poison—it hurts the one who holds it. If my mind is a room, I am shutting the door to negative thoughts and opening the window to positive ones.

After ruffling my hair, Danny helps Dad carry our bags upstairs, because my own arms are too sore to do it. Dad pops his head around my bedroom doorway on his way back down.

'Apparently Eamon will be home in a few days,' he says. 'And Claudia says we're welcome to come back and stay any time the cabin's free.'

'Like next week?' I say.

'As soon as we can, champ. I want to see him again too. That last image we had . . .'

Dad shudders, and I see Eamon again. White face, purple lips, the whites of his eyes showing, Dad pumping at his chest.

'The holidays are in a couple of weeks. If Eamon's back home, we could go visit,' Dad suggests.

'The day he gets out?'

'We might need to give them a day to get settled in. Do we look too keen if we go the day after?'

I grin. 'Dad, you've looked too keen since the first moment you saw her.'

'Was it that obvious?'

'Only to the whole village.'

Dad doesn't seem to appreciate my joke.

'But really, you like her, don't you?'

I think of Claudia's gentle smile, her long braided hair, her soft, clear voice. How she is somehow both delicate and strong.

'I really like her, Dad. Not sure how you two are going to make it work between Pleasantville here and the wilderness of mountain life, though. Unless you want to move there after all?'

Dad laughs. 'I've not long had my first kiss from her, champ.

I haven't given much thought yet to living arrangements.'

But he's smiling like a kid who just won a prize. And, again, he didn't say no. Stranger things could happen than us moving to Matilda Mountain. Stranger things already *have* happened.

Dad leaves me to unpack my stuff, but the first thing I do is stick my paintings on the wall above my bed. Not that I'm at risk of forgetting Tilly's Hut and the forbidden caves. But I need to keep them close.

I finish unpacking my suitcase, then I hover at my desk. My phone is still charging where I left it.

It feels like an artefact from another life. I'm a bit scared to turn it on. Do I want to reconnect with my old world? Not really. I feel disconnected from all of it. But I know I can't hide away forever. Hiding is no way to live.

So I turn my phone on.

A ton of messages start buzzing through. Mostly from Anna. I smile as I scroll through them.

Anna

Missing you xx

When are you back?

Enough of the mountains already!

The message that surprises me most, though, isn't from Anna. It's from Pippi.

Pippi

I'm so sorry for what I said, Scarlett. It was very unkind of me. I didn't mean it. x

I think about telling her that what she thinks doesn't matter to me. I'm more than her thoughts and I don't need to live my life impressing people like her. I'm the only person I need to make proud.

But Pippi will learn her lesson in her own time. Like the rest of us learn ours. It's not my job to teach her.

Scarlett

Thanks. See you at school.

I'm back at school in time for the School Spectacular audition, and I still look the same. There has been no magical transformation of my skin. There are limits to plastic surgery, and no amount of mineral water, photo filters, pills or potions can change that. My face tells a story. Not one I wanted it to tell, but a story that will be with me all my life. The kids at school still stare at me. They still whisper. I guess they always will. Not everyone has been burnt alive.

I can't change the accident. That happened. Maybe I've spent the last year waiting for someone to save me . . . the plastic surgeon, Dad, Nikki, Matilda Mountain. But nobody is coming to save me, because only I have the power to do that. Only I can change what happens next. And I plan to.

So I block out what everyone else thinks of me as I pull on my leotard. My arms are on full display. There is no hat to hide my face behind. My hair is pulled back in a bun, showing every little scar. But if scars are stories, then I need to wear mine the same way Dad wears his tattoos. They belong to me now. I own them as much as I own myself. And there are parts inside me that I don't like and parts outside me that I don't like, but there are more parts I do like. And I'm learning to like them more every day. I am the same me I was before, but also a different me. And I will keep being different versions of me as I grow. And that's okay. Because I wasn't put here to be Pippi or Anna or anyone else. I was put here only to be me.

My scars are my warrior marks, best worn with pride. They show how my character was painfully moulded and I won't live the rest of my life being ashamed of them. Or ashamed of who I am. Because I'm not broken, not ugly, not disfigured. I am more than one car accident. More than one fire. More than the scars I wear.

I am a survivor.

I tie the ribbons of my pointe shoes up my legs, then take my position, tucked up in a ball on centrestage.

The audience is packed with kids. Most I know. They hush at the sight of me. And right up in the front row, there is Gran. Come to see my return to the stage. Her girl, who isn't perfect, but is going to dance the legs off this song anyway.

Strangely, where I expected to be filled with knee-trembling terror, I am calm. I have survived some very real things. Dancing on stage doesn't rank as high on my terror scale anymore. Life is about taking chances, and I never did get to sit that ballet exam. But I can do this.

I still don't know if my arms will behave. A flicker of fear prickles my neck. Are my muscles strong enough to pull me through this entire dance? But I shut the door on self-doubt.

I remind myself what my arms have done already—climbing mountains, and rowing, and reeling in fish. These same arms pulled a boy from a raging, swollen river and saved his life. These are strong arms. Arms to be proud of.

The music starts. *Bird Set Free.* The girl struggling to sing, too broken to fly. And the girl is me. Too broken to dance. And she's the little bird-girl in Tilly's story.

If it was Tilly's writing that saved her, maybe it will be my dancing that can save me.

And as the song plays, I slowly unfurl from my ball, stretching up to my full height.

I dance fearlessly. Not to please a crowd, not to score well, but because I want to. Because it brings me happiness. Because dancing is a verb and I am a dancer. Even if people stare at me, even if I'm scarred and nowhere near perfect, even if I dare not to look the way the world tells me I should. I won't apologise for any of it. I am my own kind of dancer now. I exist. As I am allowed to.

I imagine myself back up on the ridgeline of Tilly's Hut, silhouetted against a rising sun in a bleak morning sky. I lift one leg up to my ear and back down. I leap like the deer by the stream. I am dancing for me. I am the little bird-girl. I stretch my arms out either side of my body. I am not just going to dance, I'm going to fly.

NOW

Miss French,

You asked me to write what I'm most scared of and, at the time, I couldn't.

Pippi told you I was scared of fire, because Pippi likes to tell people's stories her own way. But my story isn't Pippi's to tell. It might be written across my face for all the world to see, but it will never be anyone else's story. I need to learn to tell it myself.

So here goes:

My name is Scarlett. I am a fourteen-year-old survivor.

I was trapped in a burning car on the side of the Mitchell Motorway when I was thirteen. The inferno very nearly killed me, only it didn't. Instead, it melted my skin. Please don't mistake this for melting my soul. My soul is still very much alive.

When the rescuers pulled me from the burning car to save my life, the skin on my arms slid off and my muscle tissue was badly damaged. Please don't mistake this for weakness. I have worked very hard for my strength.

Pippi was right about one thing: I should be scared of fire. There are many things I should be scared of, but I try not to be. Because I have

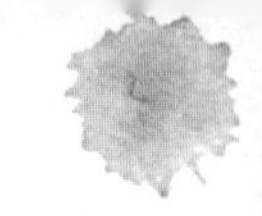

brushed my fingers across the face of death and found that life can be the scarier option. Dying is easy. It's closing your eyes and surrendering. But living? That's a daily battle.

Before the accident, I wore a mask of make-up and painted smiles. Afterwards, I wore a compression mask. Now, I wear my scars.

I think lots of people hide behind masks because they're scared of not being perfect. But I've lived long enough in a perfect world and it's only been a prison, where I am kept behind the bars of other people's thoughts. Where I am expected to have perfect skin and perfect hair and perfect make-up and a perfect body with a perfect smile to cover my perfectly unique soul.

And it turns out I prefer things not being perfect. Like a scarred tree trunk after a lightning strike, and the wonky little cabin on Matilda Mountain, and the ancient stalagmites in the forbidden caves. I like that Anna has a mole above her top lip, and that Dad's face has creases, and Eamon's ears stick out just the right amount.

I might never love my scars, but I will do my best to wear them. Because these arms and this face, changed by fire, are part of who I am now. And my scars are stronger and tougher than the skin I had before. A bit like me. My body was broken by fire, but not my spirit. And sometimes the thing that breaks you down is the very same thing that rebuilds you.

I'm not the pretty girl anymore, but I'm not the burnt girl either. I am more than both of those things. I am the girl who survived. The pretty Scarlett was nice to look at. But Scarlett the survivor, Scarlett who has lived through fire, she's brave and strong and kind of incredible. And I'm a little bit proud of her. She's someone I can grow into.

So what am I most scared of? No, it's not fire. And it's not ugliness. 'Ugly' has no place in the natural world. It turns out that living in a world of perfection scares me more than anything else.

EPILOGUE

At the base of the stairs to the city hospital, the monstrous brick building spreads its dark shadow over Dad and I. The same hospital I spent over three months of my life in. Some people never walk out of those automatic glass doors, but I did.

Dad stops at the base of the stairs. 'Memories, huh?'

I pull my courage around me like a cloak and start up ahead of Dad. He follows.

Everywhere, there are reminders.

Through the glass doors, and I'm in the stretcher bed again, ambos pushing me through to Emergency.

Inside now, and the smell of hospital-grade antiseptic hits my brain. It is dressings being torn from my flesh. It is sweating and screaming with pain.

I stop. Steady myself against the wall.

'Okay, champ?'

I close my eyes, breathe.

'Take your time.'

Open my eyes again.

We keep going. Past the florist with its sickly pungent smell of lilies. The school sent me lilies. My friends sent me lilies. White lilies with rust-coloured stamens, dull pink lilies, wilting lilies, sweet with decay. Lilies are pain.

In the big lift, Dad presses the button to the next floor. Exactly like the lifts the orderlies wheeled me into before and after surgeries. Lifts long enough to fit beds on wheels.

Down the hallway, past the physiotherapy department. Where hour upon hour, day upon day, I relearnt basic skills. Swallowing, talking, pinching my fingers together. I'm tempted to walk back through those doors. See if any of the physios that worked with me are there. Say, 'Remember when I couldn't feed myself?' But it's not them I came to see, so we push on.

Past the café that drip fed Dad coffee during our months here. Where Dad tried to coax me into having a milkshake with him, but I refused to be seen in public.

Then there is no more walking. Because we're standing outside the Respiratory Ward.

Dad and I enter together.

The ward is whisper quiet, walls bland. We follow the room numbers down a white-walled corridor until we're standing outside room 6B. A plain white door with plain black lettering on it. Housing the person I most want to see in all the world.

Dad knocks gently. I never knew his gnarled fists could hit anything so softly.

But it must be loud enough. Because before long, the handle is twisting, the door opening. And there is a face. Thin, but smiling, creases of happiness around her eyes. Long braid drooping over one shoulder, reaching halfway down the buttons on her white peasant dress.

'Well, hello,' she says, opening the door wider to reveal a blue-curtained bed.

'Claudia.' Dad's smile is a bit stiff, but he opens his arms and she steps into them. He pulls her close, and they stand there a moment, not speaking, his lips pressed against her hair.

The room is small and close and white, with one narrow window looking out over a patchwork of grimy rooftops. This room is fit for scientists in lab coats, not fish boys. Fish boys belong in cave pools and wild streams beneath beating winds.

'You can go see him, sweetie,' Claudia says, pulling away from Dad. 'I only closed the curtain because he's sleeping.'

I realise I'm just standing there, staring. I remember what it's like to be on the inside of that blue curtain. The burning pain. The cannula in my arm. The dressings on my face. The tube down my throat.

This time, though, I am not the patient. I am the survivor. The visitor. The one coming to help heal the broken.

I step forward tentatively. The last image I have of Eamon flashes across my mind. The whites of his eyes, the purple of his watery lips.

Claudia gently peels back the curtain.

Eamon's eyes are closed. Two clear tubes run from a machine by his bed into his nose. His lips are pink and dry. His dreadlocks tied neatly to one side.

He looks small in the bed. The blanched sheets are pulled to his chest, and his arms rest gently on top of them. His hands are tanned against the bleached white of the bed, and his nails have been scrubbed clean. He looks fragile. Not tough, like the boy who jumped out of a tree to greet me, or rowed a boat with me through a supercell storm.

'He's still on oxygen,' Claudia says, 'but the fluid in his lungs is clearing and his oxygen levels are almost back to normal. He's going to be fine.' She smiles at him and a tear rolls down her cheek. When she looks at me, her eyes are ancient. 'I knew the moment I met you that you were special. I just had this feeling. I knew you were meant to cross paths with us. There's something about a person who has known suffering that sets them apart.' She nods, and more tears run down. They splash onto Eamon's hand, and she wipes them away. 'I owe you, both of you, my boy's life. Without you . . .'

She bites her lip. Looks out the slit of a window and smiles.

'You are welcome any time on our mountain, okay? You and your dad. You're part of our family now.' She smiles shyly. 'You will always have a place out there. And when Eamon's back home, we'll put on a feast. Celebrate all that we have.' She turns to Dad. 'Will you bring her? Often?'

Dad's face flushes. 'I'll bring her as often as you like.'

Claudia smiles, then touches Eamon's shoulder. She gives it a gentle squeeze.

'You have some visitors, Eam.'

He opens his eyes, squinting up at us. A lazy smile breaks across his face.

'Why don't you sit down,' Claudia says to me, patting a space on the bed beside Eamon. 'You two don't need to be shy, not after what you've been through.'

So I sit beside him.

'Hi.'

We smile awkwardly at each other. There's so much to say, and all of it too hard to put into words.

'Go on and hug her, Eam. You owe this girl your life.'

Eamon sits up, and I lean over. We hug for a moment. I think about the last time I saw his body, limp in the mud. To hold him now and feel his warm back, even just for a second, is something I didn't expect I'd ever get to do after that long, cold, dark night.

When we separate, he says, 'So I hear you pulled me from the water.'

'I almost didn't.'

'But you did. You wouldn't have let me go. No way.' He grins.

He has no idea how close I came. How much strength it took not to.

'You know, you're pretty impressive for a city girl. Wildly daring for sure. You've now officially survived a fire *and* a flood.'

'Well, you were pretty *un*impressive for a fish boy,' I joke. 'Fish are not meant to drown. Can you remember that for next time?'

'Definitely.'

We laugh.

'I guess life's tried to kill us both now, huh?' he says.

'And failed.'

'Yeah, there's too much to live for. No quick departures for us.'

And I realise Eamon is right. I don't want to die a pretty girl. I want to live, however that comes. My scars may be three layers of skin deep, but my arms? They're strong and getting stronger.

And that strength will carry me through the rest of my life.

'I think we're in this life business for the long haul,' I say.

ACKNOWLEDGEMENTS

My first job as a lawyer was working in motor vehicle accident claims. I was shocked to discover the number of people in Australia left with catastrophic, life-altering injuries following a car accident. In the news, you mostly hear only of fatal car accidents, not those which leave people devastated in a multitude of other ways. I read many reports from psychologists detailing the flow-on effects of lifelong injuries on people's lives, both physically and mentally. Most of these people were adults, but there were also many children. In writing *Skin Deep*, I wanted to examine the effects of a life-altering injury in the life of a young girl.

Why a young girl? Well, I have five of them myself. And I often find myself worried about the heavy pressure society (and social media) places on girls to be perfect and beautiful. Girls are taught the value of beauty from a young age in a lot of implicit ways. Young girls are complimented first on their looks, and second on their other attributes. 'Your hair looks so pretty.' 'What a beautiful fairy dress you're wearing.' 'What a gorgeous picture you painted.' 'What a lovely tower you built.' We don't say these things to boys.

We don't constantly comment on their appearance. But we fill our girls' minds with beauty-loaded messages from infancy. And those messages carry through into womanhood. 'Be pretty. Be perfect. Be beautiful.'

But what if a girl bucks the trend? What if a catastrophic injury changes her face so drastically, she no longer recognises herself and ultimately dares to deviate from the task society has set her to be perfect? What if girls learn to value strength, grit and determination above beauty?

For those who want to dig deeper into the topics addressed in *Skin Deep*, I would recommend the following further reading:

- *Beauty* by Bri Lee
- *Unmasked* by Turia Pitt
- *Back From the Dead: Peter Hughes's Story of Survival and Hope After Bali* by Patrick Lindsay.

In exploring the above concepts in *Skin Deep*, I relied on a number of people, who I'd like to thank.

Firstly to my publisher, Scholastic Australia, thank you for giving me the opportunity to write about a topic very dear to my heart and for embracing the idea enthusiastically! Thanks also to Lorae Harbottle-Purs, for your very thorough editing and for taking on *Skin Deep* as a project close to your heart.

Thanks as always to my incredibly supportive agent, Clare Forster. These have been unprecedented times to write through, and you have been nothing short of amazing. May we work together on many more books!

To my sensitivity readers (you know who you are), thank you for reading my manuscript and guiding my representation of life with a disability, particularly with regard to facial conditions and autism. Your suggestions were invaluable.

A special thanks goes out to Mia Lawrence, for helping me name Danny and Scarlett's dad during a late-night creative writing session. Also to Milly McGrath for naming Cat.

Thanks to dear friends who really had my back through the process of writing this novel. Nicole Hamilton, your encouragement and time in reading the manuscript was the inspiration I needed to keep going. You have no idea how much that helped. Allayne Webster, the way you've supported my writing has truly astounded me. You are a rare gem and I cannot wait to meet in the flesh. Eleni Hale, we need another writing retreat! I can't wait for your next novel. Brighid Armgardt, for sharing our most intimate lives with each other. Friendship doesn't come any deeper. Also to the friends who have stood the test of time for me—Leah Warren, Sharon Lee, Tara Abell, Kate Perkins, Amanda McDermott, Jen Rickard, Kerrie Gee and Jan Moulay. Thank you for being smiling, loyal faces, for tolerating my absences when I write and for championing my work.

To Jamie Johnston, thank you for being a quiet place of refuge through my own supercell storm. Your integrity and gentle spirit continue to amaze me. As Claudia said about Eamon, you're as good as they come! Thanks also for answering my questions about supercells and weather patterns.

Thank you to Chad Lawrence, for being an amazing father to our girls. For teaching them to kickbox and surf and SUP, and for taking them on countless adventures for only the wildly daring or the wildly desperate.

To my family, I can never repay or thank you for all your support, especially the last few years. You have all stood up to be counted for me when I needed it most. To my dad, Ian O'Connor, for being only ever one call away. I can't fathom a day when you won't be on the other end of a phone for me. And to my mum, Karen O'Connor, you are the safest place for the weary to rest. You bring me sunshine, and all who know you, love you. The world needs you cloned.

To my sister, Shelley Flanders, the yin to my yang—wow, haven't we been through some times! Thank you for helping me to see new ways and new paths, and for your belief in rainbows. Your faith in life is amazing. And to my sister, Brooke Zammit, for being excited about my novels and supporting me in my writing and in my life.

Finally, to my best work. The ones I would go to the ends of the earth for. Mia, your intelligence, art and maturity have amazed me since you were a baby. I enjoy your company so much and know we'll get along well as adults. Zara, your determination, courage and resilience are inspiring. I love watching you tumble and run and kick your goals. Sophie, you're such a giver; easy-going, nurturing and selfless. Also a graceful dancer, like Scarlett! Very easy company to keep. Heidi, if kindness were a person, then I've found her. Your heart is so soft and sensitive, and there's not a mean bone in your body—you are a gift to everyone you love. And Lacey, my adventurous little gypsy, who sleeps with her sisters and loves the great outdoors. You charm everyone you meet with your wild spirit. I'm so grateful to have my own pack of little women.

ABOUT THE AUTHOR

Hayley Lawrence has been writing since she learnt to hold a pencil. She is currently a lawyer in coastal NSW where she lives with her five beautifully wild daughters and writes novels. Hayley's work is haunted by the stories she encounters as a lawyer, through her daughters and in the incredible people who lay their souls bare to her. Hayley's novels have won fellowships and been shortlisted for the Vogel Literary Award. Her work has also received critical acclaim with the Children's Book Council of Australia and the Sisters-in-Crime Davitt Award.